WEDDING CAKE CARNAGE

MURDER IN THE MIX 11

ADDISON MOORE

MURDER IN THE MIX

ADDISON MOORE

Wedding Cake Carnage

CHAPTER 1

Missing: Judge Essex Everett Baxter
Black hair, blue eyes, mid-thirties
If you have any information, contact the Ashford Sheriff's
Department.
$100,000 Reward

I see dead people. Mostly I see long gone furry creatures, but on the rare occasion I do see a dearly departed of the human variety. However, right now, my mind is drifting to terrifying places, and I can't see a thing.

"Have you seen this man?" My voice is hoarse, raw from crying, lack of sleep, and a growing desperation.

The young man before me grabs a protective hold on his fiancée as he leads her away from the table.

"*Lottie Lemon*," Lily Swanson is quick to scold me. "Would you stop that? It's bad enough you brought his picture. And a sixteen-by-twenty? It looks like you're about to eulogize the poor guy."

"Eulogize?"

My thoughts grow dark, and suddenly the din of voices, the elegant jazz music playing on blast, and the sporadic explosions of laughter all around me disappear as that fog I've been stuck in for the last nine days slowly pulls me back into its cryptic arms.

"Would you stop?" Keelie swats Lily with a stack of pamphlets she printed up that advertise the Cutie Pie Cakery and Bakery. "You're sending her over the edge again."

"Oh, I am over the edge," I assure them both as I step back from the table before us laden with an exact replica of what my sister Lainey's wedding cake will look like—

three tiers and a lavender marbled coating with thick gold icing dripping from each layer. Next to that sits a cake made entirely out of glazed donuts drizzled with white and pink frosting, and next to that is a cupcake tower frosted in the softest shade of blue. Each display is beautiful, *spectacular*—and honestly, a meager offering of what I'm capable of, considering the fact we're smack in the middle of a bona fide bridal expo. Not even the heavenly scent of vanilla and sugar can pull me out of my funk.

The Ashford Convention Center is filled to the brim with future brides, bridesmaids, mothers of the bride, single women with a dream in their heart—and every now and again, I spot the ever so reluctant soon-to-be groom.

It's wall-to-wall merchants in this cavernous space, offering a rainbow of services—photographers, videographers, vendors who specialize in booking live bands and DJs, stores that specialize in invitations and top-of-the-line stationary, and jewelers showing off their finest baubles—apparently, diamond encrusted tiaras are on order if you're to keep up with the latest bridal trends. There's a booth offering limos and other forms of snazzy transportation, three or four booths for honeymoon and travel, and a dozen beauty vendors and makeup artists—heaven forbid the bride apply her own lip-gloss. There are even a few vendors just like myself who made the trek here from Honey Hollow—just a short thirty-minute drive down the highway.

The Honey Pot Diner is here offering their catering services, and the Scarlet Sage Boutique is also present with Scarlet herself on hand offering huge savings for any gowns purchased at the expo today—and she's hauled down enough to outfit every bride this side of the continental divide.

My friend, Felicity Gilbert, has one of the most popular booths at the expo with the business she took over once her mother died, The Enchanted Flower Shop. She's created a monstrous floral arch comprised of peach and cream-colored roses, and it looks straight out of a fairytale. Even Cascade Montgomery from the Busy Bee Crafts Shop showed up for the event, offering custom made reception memorabilia such as tiny Mason jars filled with twinkle lights and other adorable trinkets.

But I can't focus on how spectacular everything looks or how pristine and perfect it all feels in this plastic wedding bubble. My mind keeps flitting back to Everett and that horrible day I found out he was missing.

I was visiting my mother's bed and breakfast not too long ago. She was throwing a relatively small victory party for Mayor Nash. Carlotta Sawyer, my biological mother who abandoned me at birth on the floor of a fire station twenty-seven years ago, was there and she was visibly shaken and angry.

Carlotta came back into my life about six months ago, and up until then I was quite content not knowing anything about her. Miranda and Joseph Lemon raised me, along with my sisters Lainey and Meg, and I couldn't have asked for a better family. I knew I was adopted, but I never felt the need to pry much deeper. The only things Carlotta left me with at the time of her departure were a blanket and a note that requested I be named Carlotta. Of course, my mother—Miranda Lemon—complied and quickly nicknamed me Lottie. Years later, Joseph Lemon died, and my mother became both mother and father to her three daughters. She made sure each of us girls stayed on the straight and narrow and even went off to college when the time came. To keep herself occupied, she purchased a run-down B&B and turned it into the gem it is today. It's haunted, of course, but that's a long story and sort of my fault.

Anyway, that fateful day at the B&B, Carlotta just finished up an argument with Mayor Nash before dragging him my way and announcing he was my father—biologically speaking. Let's just say a Mack truck could have run me over, and I wouldn't have felt a thing.

Not once have I ever been curious about who my biological father might be. Carlotta knew that. She simply blurted it out to get even with Mayor Nash for the things he said to her, which apparently were not very nice. And before I could say a single word, utter a single sound, Noah—my ex-boyfriend who works for the Ashford Sheriff's Department as the lead homicide investigator—walked right over and told me the horrible news. My boyfriend, Judge Essex Everett Baxter, was missing. They found his car door ajar, his briefcase and phone thrown into nearby bushes—and that was it.

Gone.

Without a trace.

We haven't heard one peep. No one has seen him. There isn't any video footage in the parking lot of the courthouse, so unless we find Everett, it will forever remain a mystery what's happened to him.

Forever a mystery? I shake my head at my own thought.

Not on my watch.

I take another step back, and my tiny purse thumps over my spine. It's actually a small leather backpack I've been using in lieu of a traditional purse. I'd much prefer having a handbag, but since I promised Everett I'd have the gun he and Noah gifted me with me at all times, here I am, packing heat in a room filled with tulle and lace. The gun is small, no longer than six inches with the words *Glock 26 Gen 4* printed on the side.

"Lottie," a male voice calls from my right, and I startle back to life in hopes it's Everett himself. But it's not Everett.

"Noah." My heart thumps erratically as I try to stifle the spike of adrenaline from taking off full force. "For a second there I thought you were—" I stop myself just before I say his name. As painful as it is to look at his picture, saying his name is ten times harder.

Noah comes around the table covered in a frilly pink cloth and offers me a firm embrace. And just like that, I spot a half dozen women glancing our way.

Noah is a looker, tall, built like a linebacker, black hair that turns fire red in the sun, emerald green eyes, and dimples for days. He and Everett were actually step-brothers for a brief period of time back in high school. Noah's father swindled Everett's mother out of quite a bit of money. But perhaps even more damaging to their relationship was the fact Noah saw fit to steal Everett's girlfriend at the time, Cormack Featherby. And ironically, Cormack Featherby is now in hot pursuit of Noah after all these years, even though he's tried everything to shake her.

Noah and Everett are a little less than five years older than me, both in their thirties.

Noah and I dated for a time. We were hot and heavy and I even hoped we would get engaged, but his wife came back into the picture and ruined that good time.

You see, Noah never really got around to that tiny matrimonial detail, and I dropped him like a hot potato once I realized he was not only married, but his wife wanted to reconcile. However, Noah is still very much in love with me. His divorce is pending, and I'm now seeing Everett—that is, if I ever really do see him again.

Noah pulls back and offers a mournful smile, one he's been giving me ever since Everett disappeared. Even though Everett and Noah have been warring over me—ridiculous, I realize this—Noah has put aside his differences with Everett and is doing everything he can to help find him. And, considering we've gotten absolutely nowhere, that doesn't amount to much.

The photographer's booth down the way ignites in a spray of blinding flashes of light. A white beast of a dog strides by and I try to get a better look at it, but the crowd edges in and—oh my word, that's no dog. That's a white exotic tiger. My mouth falls open as I crane my neck, but I lose sight of the magnificent beast.

"How are you holding up?" Noah dips in to catch my gaze, and I close my eyes a moment.

"Please, it's a circus in here with the blinding light and the animals roaming free. I can't believe I pushed myself to do this."

"You had to." Keelie pops over. Keelie is a gorgeous, perky blonde whom I've known since preschool and we've been best friends since. "Lottie, I couldn't let you stay in bed much longer."

"You slept in for the first seven days." Lily clicks her tongue. "You're lucky you had Margo willing to open up the shop and bake for you."

Margo is a five-star chef who works at the restaurant conjoined to mine called the Honey Pot Diner. Keelie happens to manage the Honey Pot and graciously lent me Margo for the week.

"I wasn't in bed. I was pounding the streets looking for him. Ask Noah. He was right there with me."

"That she was." He takes a deep breath. "But I'll admit, it's good to see you back in action." He glances at the myriad of cake samples being snatched up at record pace. "What have we got here?"

Lily hops over to the miniature sampler plates set out. "Coconut cake, raspberry and white chocolate, Bavarian cream—my favorite, lemon cake—perfect for summer weddings, chocolate fudge cake, pink champagne cake—yes, made with real champagne, red velvet, hazelnut vanilla, and we've got two dozen additional flavors that the happy couple can choose from." She hops up on the balls of her feet and cranes her neck as she looks in the distance. "And before I forget to tell you, A Cake Above Bakery is here, too. They're advertising installation pieces, Lottie. They actually have cakes suspended from the ceiling. We really need to up our game. Do it for Essex. He would have wanted you to."

I can't help but frown when she uses his formal moniker. Everett was quite the ladies' man before we

9

got together. And every single lady whom he happened to hit the mattress with has come away with the privilege of calling him by his proper first name. He's not that crazy about his formal name, though.

Everett comes from money, thus the one hundred thousand dollar reward his mother quickly ponied up. My goodness, his mother and sister have all but gone insane over his disappearance. They wanted to offer far more money—into the millions—but Noah cautioned against it in the event this was a money grab.

Personally, I don't think it was a money grab. Just weeks prior to his disappearance, a strange woman came snooping around Honey Hollow looking for Everett, spying on the two of us. She left a bouquet of black roses on his porch one night and a black paper heart attached to his windshield. On the day he disappeared, she left a black paper heart on my desk in the bakery with the words *he's mine* scrawled across the front. It's clear a deranged lunatic has him, and I have a feeling no amount of money could pry him out of her psychotic little hands.

My eyes snag on his framed picture. Everett is far too handsome for it to ever be legal. Hair black as night. Eyes the color of the deepest part of the ocean. He's serious, and loyal, and far too sexy to ever be safe—as evidenced by his abduction. Every woman with a pair of functioning ovaries pays him his due attention, and apparently, this woman, whoever she is, was one of them.

Noah gets right to testing out each and every flavor just as Jana March comes up, hand in hand with a tall man with light brown hair and a boyish face. He's dressed in a mint green polo and chinos, and he has that wealthy preppy vibe about him.

"Hello, Jana." I muster all the smile I can afford. "Don't tell me. You're hiding from my sister so soon?" I'm teasing. Jana is Lainey's wedding planner, and my big sister has been a bit of a bridezilla as of late. Lainey and her fiancé, Forest Donovan, are both here and have been making the rounds. They said they'd be back to do an official cake tasting in just a bit.

Jana tips back her dark hair. "Lainey is no trouble at all." Jana looks gorgeous in a flowing pink dress with gold lame flowers pressed into the fabric. Her eyes squint tightly whenever she smiles. She's the nicest person on the planet, and thankfully so since she deals with ornery brides-to-be for a living. "Lottie, this is my fiancé, Pierce Underwood. He owns Underwood Investments. You've probably heard of it. It's his first time at one of these events, so I thought I'd bring him to your booth first. There's a direct line to his happiness, and it's right through his stomach. Believe me, nothing could make him happier than to taste your samples."

"Please, help yourselves." I extend a hand his way, and he offers a hearty shake. "Lottie Lemon. I own the

Cutie Pie Cakery and Bakery. And if you find something you like—or not, I'd be happy to work with you on making all of your wedding cake dreams come true." It comes out without an ounce of emotion, wooden as if I just read it off a script, and technically I did—the pamphlet in front of me that we've been passing out by the dozens.

"That's very nice of you." He picks up a plate of coconut cake and moans through a bite. "Wow. You just knocked it out of the park with my first bite. But, of course, I'll have to try them all just to be sure."

We share a warm laugh as a young girl about my age saunters up and screams with delight once she spots Jana, and the two of them exchange a quick embrace. She's a little shorter than Jana with long dark hair that's wild and curly. She has large green doe eyes and lashes that look as if they're an inch long at least.

Jana leans my way with tears glistening in her eyes. "Lottie, this is my best friend, Jackie. She's the one that set me up with Pierce to begin with."

"*Ah*—so you're Cupid," I say, extending my hand.

"Jackie Nagle." The girl's handshake is icy and limp. "Pierce is my boss, and there's a strict no dating clause in my contract. So, I thought, heck, if I can't have him, I'll toss him to my bestie!" She snorts as she laughs, and she and Jana laugh all the more because of it. "Anyway, they clicked right away. The wedding is set for next June. Jana is booking only the best."

Jana nods frenetically, her eyes set wide as if she were trying to convince me. "I'm booking Lottie for sure. Her cakes are to die for." She quickly hands Jackie a plate and snaps up one for herself, but before she can take a bite, a redhead with a look of rage in her eyes comes this way. Jana clicks her tongue. "And here we go."

"Jana." The redhead blinks a smile over her face. "Can I speak with you for a moment?"

"Sure thing." Jana glances back my way. "This is Amanda Wellington. She's an event planner from Ashford."

"A little friendly competition, huh? I like that." I'm about to introduce myself, but the redhead has already navigated Jana into the crowd.

Pierce and Jackie wander off to the next booth, and I watch as they lean in close as if they were having a private conversation of their own.

"He seems like a good man," I say to Keelie and Lily. "And I'm glad about it, too. Jana deserves the very best."

Noah steps up and opens his mouth as if he's about to say something before he does a double take at the table and nearly jumps over Lily as he retrieves another slice of cake.

He glances around quickly as if he were shaken.

"Whoa," I say, pulling him in. "It looks like someone likes the chocolate fudge."

Noah yanks his plate back as if he were afraid I was

about to cram my face into it and devour it. "I'll be right back, Lottie. Promise me you'll stay right here." Noah hurdles over the ice chest next to me as he dives into the crowd.

"What in the heck was that about?"

Lily bumps her shoulder to mine. "I don't know, but rumor has it, Detective Fox has been spending the night at your place."

Keelie nearly gags as she plucks the fork from her mouth. "Lottie Lemon! Why do you always keep the juicy details away from me?"

"That's because they're not juicy," I say, handing her another slice of raspberry vanilla cake. "Noah has been sleeping on the couch. He doesn't like the fact that whoever took Everett knows where I work and live. I can assure you, it's been perfectly platonic." It has. Noah has been picking up a pizza from Mangias every night and we talk about how we might go about finding Everett. And when there's a bump in the night, I don't worry about it because I know Noah sleeps with one eye open and a finger on the trigger of his gun. I'm sure Everett would appreciate knowing that I felt safe at night. "Hey, Keelie? Would you please go get another raspberry vanilla cake out of the van? The box should be marked," I say, giving her the keys, and she's quick to take off.

A man in a suit walks by the booth with a couple of miniature poodles on a leash. There's a sign sandwiched over his chest that reads *rent a lovable fur creature to walk your rings down the aisle in style.*

"What do you think of that?" Lily shudders as if it didn't sit well with her.

"I think it's adorable. In fact, if I could train Pancake or Waffles to do something like that, I think it'd make my whole wedding." Pancake and Waffles are my adorable Himalayan cats. Both have cream-colored fur, a rust-tipped tail, and eyes of the bluest sky. "I can see why people would want to have a lovable pet at the ceremony. It would add levity and make everybody relax a bit. I know I would. But that tiger." I shake my head in dismay. "That beast was at least six feet long."

Lily bubbles with laughter. "Lottie, that was a Saint Bernard. They've been walking an entire cast of creatures past us for the last hour." Her expression dims quickly. "I just knew when Essex went missing, it would mess horribly with your mind."

Naomi trots up on a pair of heels that qualify as stilts. Naomi Sawyer is Keelie's twin sister, my cousin by proxy. She's a brunette stunner with a mean streak wider than any human measurement allows. Her hatred for me started in high school, which just goes to prove she can hold a grudge longer and stronger than most people are capable of. She's actually here manning a booth of her own today. The Evergreen Manor in Honey Hollow happens to be a premier wedding reception venue, and it just so happens to be where Lainey is having her big shindig after the ceremony.

"Please." Naomi yanks Everett's picture forward. "He's not missing. He left town just to get away from you." Her eyes flit to mine accusingly. "He's probably in Hawaii with a Mai Tai in his hand. Face it, Lottie. You smothered the man right onto the next available flight out of Vermont."

"Not true," I grit through my teeth. I'm about to let into her for being so crass when that white furry beast strides by again and every muscle in my body freezes. Keelie was wrong. That's no domestic animal. It's indeed a tiger.

The enormous creature pauses and turns its magnificent face my way. Its eyes are slate blue. Pale gray stripes run through its fur. A thunderous roar escapes it—more of a cross between a roar and a yawn—but the sound was perfectly ferocious.

"Lily, that's no Saint Bernard." My heart ratchets up into my throat, and I can hear it pulse right through my ears.

"What are you talking about?" Lily waves me off as she and Naomi start in on a conversation of their own.

The beast moves in a few steps and vocalizes as if its paying job was to put the fear of the Almighty into me. And by the way, mission accomplished.

"Oh my goodness," I hiss as I note it's not leashed, and not a soul seems to mind its menacing presence.

"Somebody help." It comes out weak as the beast lands a thick heavy paw onto the table with a thud. It tips its nose toward the chocolate fudge cake and starts licking away, but the cake doesn't seem to dissipate. I'm pretty sure chocolate isn't good for cats in general, but I'm not about to argue with it about its diet. However, I can't help but note it's not really getting anywhere with the task at hand.

Oh. My. Wow.

It looks up, and I'd bet my soul its lips just curled into a smile.

"You're one of them, aren't you?" I whisper mostly to myself.

Its paw sinks right through the table as it proceeds to stride through the furniture as if it weren't even there. It walks right through my body before slinking down the hall just as Keelie comes up.

"Oh, wow." I stagger for a minute as I struggle to catch my breath.

"Lottie? Are you okay?" Keelie does her best to hold me up as she asks.

"I'm fine. But somebody here is not." I give a quick look around.

Anytime an animal, pet as it were, comes back from the other side, it almost always means death is about to strike its previous owner.

Now if I could only figure out who that could be?

A tiger? An exotic tiger at that?

A few months back, I had to deal with the ghost of a bear—a BEAR—and come to find out, Eve Hollister's father owned a circus when she was young. It was Eve who was murdered. And that ornery bear and I worked together to land her killer behind bars. But this creature, I have no clue what the backstory on it could possibly be.

I take a deep breath as I look to Keelie. "I think I just need some air. Hey, where's the cake?"

"I couldn't figure out which one it was. Sorry." She pulls me close by the arm, the way she usually does when she has a bit of juicy gossip at the ready. "On my way out, I heard Jana and that girl that hauled her off ripping into one another. Something about a client list? I'll admit, I got waylaid a bit as I tried to listen in."

"Sounds ugly. I'll get that cake. And hey, if you see Noah, tell him I want to speak with him before he leaves."

I glance back and spot Ivy Fairbanks—*Detective* Ivy Fairbanks, Noah's partner at the Ashford Sheriff's Department—standing by the photographer's booth with her arms firmly folded, her gaze dead set on me. Ivy is a gorgeous redhead whom I've long suspected has more than a platonic interest in Noah.

"Huh. I wonder if Noah is having me watched?" I shake my head. "Of course, he is. This whole thing with Everett has him spooked, and rightly so. I'll be right back. Man the fort for me?" I ask while taking the keys from her, and Keelie happily obliges.

As soon as I get that cake back to the booth, I'll take off and explore the expo to see if I can find that glorified cat once again. It was a beautiful beast. A boy judging by the junk dangling as it took off in haste. As much as I don't want to get near it, I do want to see if it's following anyone. It sure seemed as if it were looking for whomever it came for.

I head down the hall that separates the back of the convention center from the party going on inside and the din of voices grows smaller and smaller. A part of me wondered if I'd bump into Jana and her angry friend, but it looks as if that good time is over for now. Not that I mind. The last thing I want is to get mixed up in something else. In fact, if I do see that ferocious poltergeist milling about, maybe I'll just go the other way. I have my hands full with finding Everett. The last thing I need on my plate is a homicide investigation.

Every muscle in my body freezes as a horrible thought comes to me.

What if it's here for Everett?

Wait a minute—it can't be here for Everett. You would think having a tiger as a pet would have come up once or twice by now. The only odd conversation we had was when he confessed that a woman who was pregnant with his child slid off an icy embankment six years ago, killing both her and the baby. That was heart-breaking to hear. Everett admitted that sadly he didn't know her too well, but he was ready to step up and be a father to that child. Nonetheless, Everett isn't physically present at this venue today. Or is he?

No, he's not. And that's exactly why I'm going to forget all about that pesky poltergeist. In fact, I'm going to spend the rest of the day minding my own business.

I head out into the scalding July sun as I make a beeline for the refrigerated van and pull out the first cake box I see. Keelie is right. They're not marked correctly. My brain has clearly taken a leave of absence. I can't blame myself too much. The stress of these past nine days has been insurmountable.

I close the van and note a small pink purse on the ground near the dumpsters.

Great. Some poor woman is probably running around frantically looking for it. I know that feeling. I've misplaced a handbag or two before I started running around with one strapped to my back. And on a day like today, I'd lose my head if it weren't attached. I usually despise that tried-and-true euphemism, but in my case, especially as of late, it's horrifically true.

I head over and balance the cake box in one arm as I lower myself to pick up the tiny pink satchel, and, as soon as I do, my eyes flit to a leg connected to a body wearing a familiar pink dress with gold lame flowers pressed into the fabric.

A scream gets locked in my throat.

Jana March lies on her stomach, her hand still clutching a fork with a bite of my pink champagne cake attached to the tines. A crimson bloom expands over her back, and a horrible groan comes from me.

Jana won't have to worry about my sister's wedding, or anyone else's wedding for that matter.

Jana March is dead.

CHAPTER 2

a scream shrills from me as I struggle to pull the phone out of my bag, and my gun tumbles out instead.

"Oh my stars," I shout as I scramble to land on it.

A crowd shuffles this way with Ivy leading the pack.

"What's happening, Lottie?" she barks it out as she yanks a weapon from the holster in her back. Ivy spots

22

the purse and trots over to the dumpster and takes a step back when she spots the body.

Within seconds, it seems as if the entire parking lot is blanketed with sheriff's deputies.

Noah runs up and helps me to my feet as I stuff my weapon back into my backpack.

"What the hell happened?" Noah takes a few steps out toward Ivy and gets a look at the grisly scene. Ivy checks Jana's vitals before shaking her head our way. "Everybody back," he shouts as a crowd begins to build. "Lottie, don't move."

Half the people here gasp my way as if I were the killer. Noah puts a call in on his phone before making his way over to me again.

"I need to get you out of here," he pants, trying to catch his breath.

"What? Don't worry about me. Worry about poor Jana. Is she really dead?"

"Yes, Lottie, she's gone." His eyes are darting every which way as if he were looking for anything suspicious he could find in the crowd. "I need to get you home, to Honey Hollow. I don't want you hanging around the convention center anymore."

"Well, I suppose the convention is over. I'll head in and start boxing up my things."

"No." His voice is a touch too loud, a touch too controlling for my liking.

"Noah? What's gotten into you? I'll be less than a

ADDISON MOORE

second. Keelie is in there. My mother and sisters are, too. I can't just leave and hope for the best."

"Look, I get it." He squeezes his eyes shut for a moment. The searing sun bears down on us a bit too hard, and suddenly I'd do anything to be back in that air-conditioned building. Killer be damned. "Lottie, I found something on your table. A black paper heart."

"*What?*" I shriek. "Is that what you were diving to get? Where is it? Can I see it? Oh my Lord, does that mean she's here?"

"I'm afraid so." He pulls out his phone. "I put the evidence in a plastic bag and it's safe in my glove compartment, but I took a picture."

I lean into the screen, and sure enough there's a black paper heart, the exact same shape and size as the one Everett found on his windshield and the one on my desk that read *he's mine.*

"What does that say?" I expand the screen until the white printing is legible. "He's happy now." An explosion of acid rips through my stomach. "Oh my goodness, she's completely nuts. Why would she do this? Why would she bother coming here and leaving this for me?"

"I think she's hoping you'll call off the search. Either that or she's gloating. I can promise you one thing—he's not happy. He is certainly not willing to be wherever it is she has him. And I hope to heaven she hasn't hurt him. Everett's a big guy. It would take a lot for an average-sized woman to restrain him."

"Hurt him?" The ground sways beneath me as I look to the deputies cordoning off the area with bright yellow caution tape. "Do you think she killed Jana?"

"At this point, I suppose anything is possible. But no, I don't have any evidence that points in that direction. Let's get you inside, Lottie. I need to help you get your things so we can get you on your way to Honey Hollow. If you don't mind, I'd like to ask Keelie or one of your sisters to stay with you until I get home."

"To what? Babysit me? No thank you."

Noah tips his head to mine, his eyes pleading for me to understand.

"Fine."

We head back into the convention center where the cool air does little to settle my jumbled nerves.

Lily and Keelie are holding themselves at the booth as the entire cavernous room seems to be aflutter.

Mom and Carlotta dart our way, looking every bit frantic.

"Is it true, Lottie?" Mom's blue eyes are twice their size. My mother is gorgeous and looks far younger than her true age should ever allow. She has a propensity to dress to the latest fashioned trends and keeps her hair shoulder length and dyed a fresh shade of butter yellow.

Carlotta, my biological mother, looks exactly like my twin with the same caramel-colored waves and hazel green eyes. Just add a few wrinkles and a handful of gray hair, and I know exactly what I'll look like in the future if I abstain from sunscreen and indulge in one too many worries.

"Yes, it's true." I bite down over my lip, suddenly wondering if we're pondering the same truths.

"Oh, thank goodness." My mother slaps her chest and bucks with all the drama she can afford. "Where did they find him? Is he here? Oh, we'll have him over for dinner tomorrow night just in time for our Nash Bash."

The Nash Bash is what she's dubbed the little meet and greet she's conducting between my newly found biological father and his children and me. I've known Mayor Nash all my life, and I happened to like his ex-wife Chrissy a whole lot more than I do him. Harry Nash is nothing but a notorious two-timer. And unfortunately for me, he's digging his two-timing claws into my mother as well. I'm secretly hoping she'll be put off by the idea of dating the person who was revealed to be my DNA donor. But according to that grin blooming on her face, it's the farthest thing from the truth.

"Mother, Everett is still missing," I say as I scoop his picture off the front of the table. I can hear Noah behind me helping Lily and Keelie shove everything into coolers.

Carlotta snaps up a couple of plates with sample pieces before Lily can toss them into the trash.

"Oh hon, don't you dare," Carlotta scolds. "This is breakfast, lunch, and dinner for me." She winks my way. "Bet you saw that hunk of burning love wandering around this place. Big blue eyes, shock of white hair, about three feet tall, six feet long."

I suck in a quick breath. "You saw him, too, huh?" And by *it*, I mean my tiger friend who was sent to assist in solving Jana's murder.

Carlotta is transmundane like me, further classified a supersensual—meaning, we can see the dead—humans and animals alike. It used to be that when they appeared it meant nothing more than a scraped knee for the person they came back for. But for the last ten months straight, they've been a harbinger for murder.

I'm not sure why I have this gift, but it turns out, my grandmother Nell Sawyer had it, too. For a long time, Nell was the only one who knew I had this gift, and it wasn't until last winter that I learned she had it as well.

Nell died in January, but she came back last month to help with Rich Dallas' murder investigation. And was I ever glad to see her. She gave me a little insight to my future, such as the fact I'll be a mother someday. She also hinted that something awful was about to happen to Everett, and boy was she right.

The other thing she mentioned was the fact my powers seem to be growing. It used to be I could only see the dead, then a few months ago I began to hear them, and the next thing I knew, they had the ability to move things in the material world—talk about a fright. One of the human ghosts, Greer Giles, was able to linger on right here on earth, and she now haunts my mother's

B&B along with her two-hundred-year-old boyfriend, Winslow Decker.

Lainey and Forest head this way, and Lainey looks as if she's seen a ghost herself. Lainey doesn't know about my gift. Only Carlotta, Noah, and Everett are apprised of my ability to see the dead—and that about puts a cap on who I'm sharing that spooktacular little secret with.

Lainey's arms flail through air. "Oh my goodness, you found the body, didn't you?" Lainey and I share the same caramel hair coloring and hazel eyes. Even though I've always known I was adopted, it was our shared looks that gave me hope that my parents had the details wrong.

"A body?" Mom pauses midflight from popping a bite of my pink champagne cake into her mouth.

Forest nods. "They found a woman outside, shot through the back. A buddy of mine just let me know." He heads over to Noah. "Are you securing the building?"

"I'm letting the deputies take care of this until I can get Lottie into her van and on her way back to Honey Hollow. In fact, I was about to ask if any of you would mind staying with her until I get home."

Carlotta moans and lifts a hand. "I'm in. Lottie and I will play gin rummy until you get back."

"No, we won't." I take a moment to glower at Carlotta. "We can snuggle with the cats and watch TV. I don't have it in me to think or play games."

Keelie wraps an arm around me. "I'm coming, too. So who did you find?"

"Yeah." Lainey leans in. "Anyone we know?"

Everything in me says run. The last thing I want to do is tell my poor stressed out sister that her wedding planner was just murdered in cold blood.

Meg comes up with her boyfriend Hook by her side. Meg is our younger sister, younger than me by a year. She's dyed her blonde locks jet-black, and it looks stunning juxtaposed against her pale blue eyes. Meg used to work the female wrestling circuit in Las Vegas for a time, but she's been back in Honey Hollow for a while now. These days she's teaching the strippers down in Leeds how to bust a move, and she's getting paid a shiny nickel doing it.

Meg slings an arm around Lainey's shoulder. "Just heard your wedding planner bit the big one." She clicks her tongue. "Let me guess, Lot. You found the body?"

A guilty look sweeps over my face, and Lainey howls so loud you'd think someone just fired a bullet into her back, too.

"Oh my goodness!" Lainey roars my way. "You are *not* permitted to come within a hundred yards of either Forest or me for the next three weeks. Do you understand?" The veins in the sides of her neck distend. Lainey has made it known in the past that she feels I might be a tad bit of bad luck when it comes to attracting the Grim Reaper.

ADDISON MOORE

She yanks Forest by the hand as they take off.

"She'll come around, Lot," Forest shouts as they make their way out of the venue.

"Wait!" Meg grabs Hook, her official boyfriend now that Keelie is out of the picture. For a while Hook was dating both of them. "Hook has some listings he'd like to share with you!"

Hook pushes out a greedy grin. "I'm the number one sales person at Redwood Realty. Anybody up for buying a house?"

Meg yanks him off before we can contemplate the advantages of having a mortgage payment with far too many zeros on the end.

Carlotta giggles up a storm as if she were a schoolgirl.

"What?" I snip, because I'm not finding a darn thing funny.

"Oh, don't mind me. It's all this yummy sugar. It's going straight to my head."

Mom threads her arm through Carlotta's. "Come on. Let's get to Lottie's and prepare the house for her. Lottie, I have the spare key. We'll have the tea on by the time you get home."

Keelie wraps her arms around me. "And I'll drive her straight there."

Both Carlotta and my mother scoop up as much cake as their arms will allow before ducking for the exit.

Lily nods. "I'll close up the bakery tonight. You just

get some rest. With Everett missing and now a body, I can't imagine what else can go wrong for you."

And like a curse from the universe, a pair of familiar blondes pop up before us. Britney Fox, Noah's legal plus one—and Cormack Featherby, the girl who is convinced she's his current fiancée.

Cormack found the engagement ring Noah bought for me in his closet last month and has taken the liberty to wear it herself. Noah tried to explain that it wasn't meant for her, but she thought he was being coy and has outright refused to take off that chunky rock that was meant for my finger.

But, as it stands, last month Everett's mother shoved her own mother's wedding ring onto my finger—and in fear of losing it, it's been warming my hand ever since.

For whatever reason, Everett thought it was a good idea to fool his mother and sister into thinking we were engaged, and we've gone along with the farce ever since.

"Noah, I believe this is your department," I say as I hand Britney a slice of chocolate fudge cake, and she gladly accepts. The scent of vanilla and cocoa permeates the air between us, and it's intoxicating. Britney owns an entire slew of Swift Cycle gyms. She's even planted one across the street from my bakery. And once her classes are over, she sends all of her clients my way as a means to cleverly replenish their calories. It's a system that works for both of us.

Britney is a sassy, sexy character who has that whole

Jessica Rabbit sultry vibe down to a science. Hair covering one eye, full lips, va-va-voom figure—check, check, and check.

"Thanks, Lou Lou," Brit says as she takes a quick bite out of the decadent cake.

Another thing that both Britney and Cormack have going is the inability to keep my name straight. But I've long since stopped correcting them.

Britney boot scoots her way to the nearest detective. "Noah, just the husband I was hoping to see. Now that our counseling is over, I think we should have dinner to discuss our future."

"Great." Noah's dimples ignite, but he's not smiling at her. "I'll be at the B&B tomorrow night, and we can do just that." In another odd twist of fate, both Britney and Cormack are staying at my mother's B&B.

My mouth opens and closes. "Noah, I thought you were having dinner with me? Trust me, I'll need you and all the high-powered weapons you can bring to protect Harry Nash from my fury. It's best I leave my weapon at home for the reunion."

"*Ooh*, I am." He winces at his wife.

"Not a problem." Britney scoops up another slice of chocolate fudge cake. "I'll simply crash the party. We're all one big happy family—right, Leslie?"

"Right." In the grand scheme of things, I'd much rather listen to Britney and Noah hash out the details of their divorce than meet another branch of my twisted family tree.

"I'll be there, too." Cormack is quick to tack on an invite of her own. "I wouldn't miss it for the world." She slaps Lily's hand from the pink champagne cake as she snatches up another piece. "I've got so many great ideas for our wedding, Big Boss. Just you wait until we pore over all this material." She holds up a Louis Vuitton tote bag bursting at the seams with all the giveaway goodies from the expo. "So many great ideas, so little time! I'll never be able to settle on just one theme. We might just have to get married *twice*. Ta-ta!" She scampers off with Britney, and I shake my head at the sight.

"How in the world did you get into that mess?" I can't help but ask the question.

Noah takes a deep breath and scratches the back of his head. "I ask myself that every day, Lottie. Every darn day." He starts in on loading up the trolley, and a sparkle of quivering light catches my eye from the next booth over. I don't hesitate heading in that direction, and sure enough there's a tiger the size of a casket slinking my way.

"Hey," I hiss over at him as I bend over. I'm terrified, but considering he's dead, I think I've got something going for me. "Here kitty, kitty." A spike of perspiration bites under my arms as the enormous creature strides forward.

His shoulders hike up and down with his every

move. He's got a mean sour puss look on his face, but he doesn't take those steely blue eyes off me. And sadly, those blue eyes remind me all the more of my own sour puss, Everett. Suffice it to say, Judge Baxter could be as ornery as the next judge, if not more so. In fact, that's how I met Everett. I was a defendant in his courtroom, and he wisely saw the light and sided with yours truly.

"Hey, sweet cat," I whisper as my voice trembles. "Do you have a name?" I do my best to scan its neck for a collar. I really don't know if you'd leash a large cat like this. In the least, I'm pretty sure a cage would be in order. When Dutch, the golden retriever that I fell madly in love with came back last December, he still had his dog tag on.

The feisty feline gets within a foot of my face and I stop breathing altogether. My word, its head is twice as big as mine. I don't care if it has sailed over the rainbow bridge, it's menacing to a fault and I'm certain I'm going to have nightmares for the rest of my natural life.

"*Rawr!*" he bellows so loud every muscle in my body freezes as the vibrations of his voice pass through me like a tuning fork. "Hello, Lottie," he thunders out the words and I gasp.

And just like that, my powers sprint in the most verbose direction of them all.

"You can talk?" I breathe a sigh of relief. "That's fantastic. Because you are going to tell me everything."

His lips curl slowly as if he were smiling, and in a spasm of light he up and disappears.

Jana March's murder investigation just got a whole lot more interesting.

And then an idea hits me.

I'm going to employ every ghost I know to help me find Everett. I don't care how many supernatural laws we'll be breaking.

Rules were meant to be broken.

And boyfriends were meant to be found.

I'm coming for you, Everett.

Just you wait and see.

CHAPTER 3

*D*inner at my mother's haunted bed and breakfast isn't usually something I dread, but on a night like tonight, one that has promised to bring forth every new relative I never really wanted to meet, it's absolute agony just walking through the door.

"You've got this, Lottie." Noah pulls me in for a quick embrace, and his familiar spiced cologne permeates me like a membrane.

"I wouldn't have anything without you—and I'm specifically referencing my sanity." I bite down over my lip as I bear into his verdant green eyes. "Partially because you forced me to show up, and partially because your support has buoyed me on during everything I've been through these past few weeks." Tears come without warning. "Thank you for that."

"Hey, it's nothing." He picks up my hand and kisses the back of it. "You're going to get through tonight like a champ. I'll be with you every step of the way."

"And afterwards, we can go back to my place and try to figure out how to get Everett back to safety." It's what we've done for the last two weeks to no avail, but it doesn't mean I'm giving up.

"That's exactly what I was thinking."

My mother's B&B is quaint, spacious, and is booked for the foreseeable future, no thanks to the haunted Honey Hollow tours she runs. Let's just say that my mother has capitalized brilliantly off the fact she has a couple of spooks running around this place.

A few months back, my mother's B&B was hurting for business, and coincidentally there was the ghost of a bear running amuck through the place while she hosted the birthday of one of her dear friends. Sadly, her friend passed away that day, and half the town is now convinced it's Eve Hollister's ghost that haunts these crooked halls, but it's not Eve Hollister at all. It's Greer Giles, a girl who perished a few months back.

Greer was in her mid-twenties, beautiful, mean-spirited, and definitely trying to sink her hooks into Everett. But all of that ended the day she was shot in the back, and she's since decided to eschew paradise and take up the challenge of haunting my mother's B&B along with her two-hundred-year-old boy toy, Winslow Decker. Greer is gorgeous with long black hair and a face that could grace any magazine cover—even in her rather deathly pale state. Winslow has light brown wavy hair and enough facial scruff to ensure he's beyond adorable. They really are a cute pair.

An ethereal glow illuminates the hall that leads to the grand room and I lead Noah in that direction. That glow is usually indicative of a supernatural presence, but instead of finding Greer Giles' smiling face or Winslow Decker's happy-to-see me countenance, I find a young girl with long dark hair covering her face, dressed in a throwback pinafore, dirty scraped knees, scuffed Mary Jane slippers—and is that a bloody knife dangling from her hand?

Something between a scream and a gasp escapes me. "Holy stars!" I howl as I bury my face in Noah's chest once again.

"What is it, Lot?" I can feel his heart begin to hammer under my cheek. "Is it the tiger again?"

"I wish!" I hiss as I summon the bravery to glance back, only to find Greer and Winslow tending to the child. Greer does her best to comb the girl's hair back while the child is busy trying to decapitate Greer as a thank you. "*Greer*!" I hustle Noah over with me, securing my hand over his so he can hear the entire conversation. A few months back, I discovered that I act as a conduit, and that if someone holds my hand, they can hear the dead, too. "What in heaven's name is going on over here?" I jump out of the way as the girl wildly brandishes the machete she's taken a serious liking to.

"Now, now." Greer licks her fingers and slicks the girl's hair away from her face, and I gasp at the sight of her. She's gorgeous. A beautiful button nose, sparkling rainbow-colored eyes, and perfect bowtie lips. She looks practically harmless now that Greer has tamed her mane. The girl stomps forward and growls out a roar that can rival any tiger on earth or in heaven.

"*Geez*." Noah jumps back, his hand disconnecting briefly from mine. "What the heck was that? Is that the lion?"

"*Tiger*. And no, it wasn't him. It's a little girl." I bend over, hoping not to startle the tiny poltergeist bent on being a menace. "What's your name, sweetie? And why aren't you in paradise?"

The little girl spikes the knife into the floor between my feet as if it were a javelin.

Winslow chortles as if it were adorable. "Just the way I taught her. We've been practicing out back all morning."

Greer takes up the little girl's hand and the little girl

scowls ten times harder. "Her name is Azalea. Isn't that beautiful?"

"*Lea*," she snips back. "Nobody dares call me Azalea."

Noah takes a breath. I can tell this is freaking him out about as much as it's freaking me out, and I should be used to all the freak-freakery that the other side can muster by now.

"Lea," I say. "That is beautiful. My name is Carlotta, and nobody dares call me anything but Lottie."

Lea's eyes grow wide. "Or else?" She looks almost amused by my proclamation.

"Or *else*," I mimic while slashing my throat with my finger. "So are you new to Honey Hollow?"

"Oh heavens no," she replies, sounding a bit more chipper and looking decidedly less deadlier than a few minutes ago. "My family was slaughtered right here over this very bed and breakfast. I've been hiding out, lying in wait, ready and willing to avenge their blood."

Lovely.

I bite down hard over my lower lip. So it turns out the B&B was haunted, after all.

"Well...I think...that's perfect, because rumor has it, Greer and Winslow here are looking to adopt. I think the three of you make a fine looking family." If your last name is Manson.

The little girl lets out another roar, albeit far more tamed. "I don't want to be *de*-dopted! I want to scare people and make them run screaming into the night. And none of these residents at this ridiculous inn are afraid of anything." She snaps her neck in Greer and Winslow's direction. "Don't you dare call yourselves ghosts. You're nothing but balls of worthless air! I can't stand either of you!" She stomps off and the floor rattles in her wake as she disappears right through the living room wall.

"Wow," I muse. "It looks like you've bypassed the toddler years and dove straight into preteens. Good luck with that. Noah and I are having dinner with my new family. Feel free to cause an electrical short that will send us running for Nash-free pastures."

"*Lottie*." Greer makes a face. Both Greer and Winslow were present when Carlotta dunked the news over my head like a platter of cold spaghetti. "They were kind enough to arrive early and they're patiently waiting for you. Your brother is a hottie, by the way. And I happened to once know both Kelleth and Aspen." Her lips curve with malicious intent. "I dare you to ask Aspen about her time at the Elite Entourage. If I'm right, she still serves her wares to men with fat wallets."

"*What?*" both Noah and I say at the very same time.

"Greer, the Elite Entourage is a glorified prostitution ring. I'm not asking my new sister if she turns tricks on the side."

In all honesty, it was Greer who used to turn tricks

on the side, and that's exactly what landed her in this ghostly predicament to begin with. Just the thought of Aspen putting herself in the same line of danger makes me shiver.

Noah leans in. "Any news on that tiger?"

I asked Carlotta to give Greer the heads-up.

"None," she says. "But as soon he shows up, I'll be the first to let you know. I'm dying to see him. Lord knows I love me a sexy cat." She lifts her shoulders in turn and Winston howls with laughter.

"Great." I'm about to take Noah and head for the dining room when a thought hits me. "Oh, and one more thing—you're both officially recruited to help find Everett."

Winslow inches back and his mouth opens, but I cut him off before he can protest.

"I don't care about the laws you're bound to. There's a missing man in this world and he belongs to me. You will help me track him down, you will walk through walls, through concrete, through continents if need be to help me get him back."

"Lottie." Greer looks affronted. "You realize we have a higher authority to answer to."

"And you realize I can have this B&B haunted by a very scary little girl who happens to wield a machete. I'm sorry to force your hand, but time is ticking and I'm terrified that if any more of it slips by, Everett will be the next to join you on your haunting spree."

A flicker of light catches my eye from down the hall and I spot Lea hiding behind a wall curling her finger for me to head her way.

"Excuse me a moment." I trot over, inadvertently leaving Noah behind as well.

"I heard you." Her nose twitches as if I let an offensive odor fly. "Call off those ninnies. They have no intention on looking for anyone outside of this B&B. I can see it in their lying souls. I'll do it for you. And I'll produce results."

"You will?" I tip my head her way, filled with suspicion.

"That's right. And in exchange you'll make sure I'm put in charge of this haunted hovel. Greedy and I Move so Slow will be given an eviction notice as my payment. I don't want them here cramping my spooky style. I'm taking over the haunting of the B&B. You know what they say—one is deadly. Three's a crowd."

"Do you really think you can bring back Everett?"

Her eyes squint as she presses out the hint of a naughty smile. "I'll bring back anyone you want me to."

"You've got a deal."

I trot back and wave to Greer and Winslow. "Never mind," I say and Noah and I head in the opposite direction.

"What happened, Lot?"

"That little spook just assured me she'd bring Everett back home to me where he belongs."

"That's up for debate—the back to your home where he belongs part," Noah mutters as we head over to the dining room.

The chafing dishes are lined up like silver orbs over the granite counter in the back. Bodies mill around, each with a drink in hand, while laughter abounds throughout the room.

"See that?" I give Noah's hand a quick tug. "They're all having a great time. They don't need us. Let's go to Mangias." I try to make a run for the door, but Noah reels me back.

"You've come this far, Lottie. I promise it'll be quick."

My lips press tight to keep from laughing. "I do believe you said those exact same words just before you frosted my cookies, detective."

A warm laugh pumps through him. "There was nothing quick about that night." His lids hood with the memory. "If you need a refresher, I'm up for it. Name the time and the place and I'm there."

"Noah." I close my eyes a moment. "If I said yes, would you get me out of there?" I cringe as Everett comes to mind. "Okay, fine," I say, cinching my grip over his hand as I stride us into the dining room as if we wanted to be there.

"You almost had me," he says. "In fact, why don't we go now?"

"Very funny."

The Nashes are here looking exquisitely expensive in their designer clothes. Their expensive perfume adds pretentiousness to the air, and for a brief second I wish I had taken Noah up on his offer.

Here goes nothing.

CHAPTER 4

"*L*ottie!" my mother screams with delight as she heads this way with Mayor Nash in tow. The entire room stills, and it's all eyes on me.

The dining room of the B&B has been transformed to look like the interior of an expensive restaurant with a white linen cloth covering the elongated table. Bouquets of spring flowers are strewn across the runner, and there are dozens of tapered candles set in my mother's finest crystal candlestick holders.

"Here she is, everyone! The woman of the hour!" My mother waves us deeper into the room. "And along with her is the handsome Detective Fox. It's a pleasure to have you both. Lottie, please, come, come. Everyone is so anxious to get to know you better."

I do a quick scan of all the familiar faces. Mayor Nash, of course, is front and center. He's tall and barrel-chested, has caramel-colored wavy hair, and a perpetual grin that I regard more as a political ploy.

His daughters, Kelleth and Aspen, are here, both blondes, both with permanent scowls and turned-up noses because they think they're better than everyone else. For sure they think they're better than me. They have for years.

Chrissy, Mayor Nash's ex-wife, waves from the back, and next to her is their son, Finn. He's tall and shares my same light brown hair and is relatively handsome in a conventional way. I don't know him that well, but what I remember of him he seemed kind and down-to-earth.

I don't suspect any of my new relatives share my supersensual standing, seeing that it stems from Carlotta, but nonetheless I'm spooked.

Mayor Nash steps forward, lumbering, a little stiff as if he were uncertain about what he was getting into. "Lottie Lemon, let me be the first to welcome you to the family."

Even though he was standing right next to me that day when I found out about my paternity, I took off rather quickly with Noah and got straight to the business of looking for Everett. And I've masterfully evaded him ever since.

"Thank you," I say as I shift my gaze to Kelleth and Aspen. "I look forward to getting to know all of you better."

Finn bounds over with open arms. "I got to get a hug from my new baby sister." He offers a warm embrace. He holds the scent of fresh pine needles and warm spices, and I like him a lot already. "I heard you have a bakery." He's beaming from ear to ear with a friendly grin, and I can't help but grin right back.

"Yes, and you're all welcome to stop by anytime."

Finn pats his belly. "You're officially my favorite sister, Lottie."

We share a warm laugh as my mother ushers us to the buffet and we quickly take our seats. Aspen openly ogles me as she chews her food.

"I hear you're quite the detective." She hikes a heavily penciled-in brow. Aspen has exaggeratingly large eyes and lips. There's a Betty Boop appeal to her, if Betty Boop were a snobby preppy—and perhaps a prostitute, too.

"That she is." Noah lifts his glass as if he were ready to make a toast to me. "Lottie has helped the Ashford Sheriff's Department on many occasions."

"Interesting," Kelleth muses. Kelleth has always had a habit of overdoing the blush, the eye shadow, and the layers and layers of lip-gloss. And sadly, that superficial layer is about all I know of her. "Daddy says your boyfriend is missing. It's nice to see you've recovered so quickly." She winks over at Noah.

"Actually, Noah and I are—"

"Just friends!" a high-pitched female voice shrills from behind as Cormack lands on the other side of Noah as subtle as a hurricane. "Cormack Featherby, soon-to-be Fox." She flashes the engagement ring she swiped from Noah. I spot Britney striding in a bit cooler than her counterpart.

"I'm Noah's wife, Britney," she says as she makes her way to the buffet, and I can't help but notice Finn just did a double take.

Hey? Maybe Finn and Britney will fall madly in love and that will finally put a nail in Noah's marital casket? Now there's a cheery thought. Noah has been emotionally out of the marriage ever since she cheated on him years ago.

"Featherby?" Aspen gawks. "You're not related to Landon by chance?"

"That's my baby sister."

"And one of my closest friends!"

Great. Cormack and my new sisters are getting along just fine. I can't help but note my own sisters—the originals—are no-shows to this unwanted family reunion.

"So, Lottie"—Finn leans in—"what happened to this judge you were seeing? One minute he's fine, and the next he disappears into thin air?"

Noah rattles off all the details as quickly as he can, and I'm thankful for it. If I start in on Everett, I might just lose it. This entire night is proving to be emotionally exhausting.

Mom jumps in her seat. "Oh, Lottie! Tell them about the latest body you found."

Kelleth's mouth rounds out in horror. "*Latest?*"

I suck in a quick breath just as Lainey and Meg stroll in.

"What did we miss?" Meg shouts as she and Lainey head for the buffet.

Mom nods her way. "Lottie was just about to tell them about the corpse she found."

Lainey whimpers into her shoulder and I want to drop into a hole. Poor Lainey shouldn't be here. She shouldn't be anywhere near me.

Meg rocks back on her heels. "Lottie finds a stiff about once a month. So all of you new siblings had better watch your back." She gives a cheeky wink, but no one seems all that amused.

In fact, Kelleth looks as if she's hyperventilating and Aspen is searching for the nearest exit.

"I'm not a killer," I say in the event they took a mental leap and went there. "In fact, I often bring killers to justice."

"Every single time." Noah is back to toasting me again.

Kelleth looks to her father. "Daddy, we've just been threatened. I no longer feel safe in her presence. You said so yourself. She's a magnet for trouble just like her mother."

Both Mom and I suck in a sharp breath.

"I meant Carlotta." Mayor Nash tosses up his hands.

Chrissy groans. "Oh, Harry. You always were an expert at putting your foot in your mouth."

"Nobody calls either of my mothers trouble," I howl. Without thinking, I pick up my water and splash it in his face. The room goes silent, save for a fearful roar, and something quickens me to turn back to the entry of the room, only to find that behemoth white tiger making his ghostly appearance. He slinks on in and hops onto the table in one lithe move, trotting across the surface, causing the dishes to rattle, glasses to topple over—and, oh my stars—utter chaos breaks out.

Kelleth and Aspen grab their purses and run screaming for the door.

"She's a witch, Daddy!" Kelleth screams from the other side of the room. "Get out while you can. We've angered her—and now all of Honey Hollow is quaking!"

Mayor Nash wipes his face down and offers an amicable smile my way. "I believe that was uncalled for —on *my* part. I owe you and both of your mothers an apology." He stands and my mother does her best to mop up the water beading down his suit.

"Oh, Harry, I'm so sorry," she pants as she does her best to clean him up.

"Don't apologize, Mother. Carlotta told me all about how he's berated her the entire time she's been back in town." I lean in hard his way. "How dare you imply she amounted to a loser. I did the math, and you were married to Chrissy when you conceived me!"

Kelleth and Aspen gasp from the door.

Mom shoots me with her crazy eyes. "That's enough, Lottie."

"Oh, it is enough." This dinner is enough. I glance to the tiger, who paused long enough to look my way as if taking in the scene. His lips curl up on the sides as he dismounts from the table, causing the back end to lift a good foot.

More screams ensue, and just about everyone is headed for the door.

"We'll get in touch soon," Mayor Nash says as he bolts for the exit.

Chrissy comes over and offers me a hug. "You are and will always be a very special girl, Lottie. You know I've loved you as if you were one of my own for as long as I've known your mother. We're family, and I'm on your side."

"Thank you for coming. You didn't have to do that."

"Not a problem." She waves to us all on her way out. "Lainey, I'm excited for the wedding!"

Lainey moans. "Wish I could say the same," she mutters.

Finn comes over and holds his arms out once again, this time with a little less conviction, but I hug him nonetheless.

"We'll do it again. This Saturday, Honey Lake. Take two will be miles better."

"Sounds good. What's Saturday?"

Noah lands a warm hand over my shoulder. "It's the Fourth of July, Lottie. I hear there's nothing like the Fourth in Honey Hollow."

"It's quite the celebration," I say. But without Everett, I'd rather hide under my covers with my cats than join in on the fun.

Mom walks them to the door as Meg and Lainey come up.

Meg gives a wistful shake of the head. "You sure know how to clear a room, Lot. And we didn't even get to the good part. How's the murder investigation going?"

My eyes meet with Lainey's, and I can hardly bring myself to hold her gaze. "It's going. Noah and I still have to formulate a game plan." I shrug over at Lainey. "Any idea who would want Jana dead?"

"None whatsoever. But one thing is for sure. I want in on this one."

"What? No," I say emphatically, rejecting her offer. "You have a wedding to take care of. And in the event you haven't noticed, you're down one wedding planner."

"I have all her notes, and the venue and musicians and florists are all booked—I think."

"But there are probably still things to do." A thought comes to me. "Forward me her notes and I'll take care of all the little details. I promise you, Lainey, your wedding will go off without a hitch." Tears come to my eyes because it's the least I could do.

Lainey bears into me with her gaze an inordinate amount of time. "Fine. But I'm recruiting Meg to work alongside you. Maybe if the two of you work together, you can make up for one professional wedding planner."

"We will." Meg salutes her. "In fact, we'll do one better. I bet Jana wasn't planning a hostile takeover of the bride the night before her wedding for a raunchy good time otherwise known as the bachelorette party."

"Oh no," Lainey is quick to protest. "You are not kidnapping me the night before my wedding."

"Fine," I say. "We'll do it a few days out." I wink to Meg. "And I'll make sure a kosher time is had by all." I turn to Noah. "Hey? Are there any male strip clubs in Leeds?"

Noah inches back. "Why in the world would you ask me that?"

Meg barks out a laugh. "I've got us covered, Lot. Don't you worry about a thing."

That ornery tiger trots back this way, and I excuse myself for a moment as I follow him out into the hall.

"Oh no, you don't," I say, grabbing him by the tail and I marvel at how soft and thick it feels. It never fails to amaze me at how solid the visitors from the other side can be.

The tiger turns my way and sheds an all-out grin. "Good show, Lottie," he growls it out low and slow.

Just hearing him say my name takes my breath away. "What's your name?"

"Beasty."

"*Beasty?*" a small voice chimes from behind. I spot Lea floating forward, her dark hair still neatly pinned behind her ears. "I rather like you, Beasty. You and I will make a fine pair."

"Well, you can't have him," I say. "Beasty was sent to help me solve a murder investigation." I look to the magnificent creature. "And, in addition to catching the killer, I want you to help me find my boyfriend. His name is Everett Baxter. He's a judge and he's been kidnapped by an insane woman who is most likely obsessed with him."

Beasty lets out something closer to a purr than a roar. "What's in it for me?"

"What would you like?" *Please don't say a nice juicy steak because I'm almost certain you won't be able to eat it.*

"To prolong my stay on the planet. My life was cut

short. I had escaped my enclosure and was shot on sight as I entered a school ground."

"Poor Beasty!" Lea hops onto his back and he gives her a friendly jostle. "And don't forget what I want, Lottie." Her eyes darken as she narrows her gaze to mine.

Lord knows I have no business making promises to ghosts, but when it comes to Everett I'd leverage my very soul if I had to.

Lea nods. "I want full run of the B&B. I want those twits you've assigned to haunt this place out of my way or under my charge. Do you understand?"

I turn and spot Greer and Winslow floating this way. "I understand."

"There you are, little one." Greer is about to take Lea by the hand but retracts as she spots the tiger. I do a quick introduction and Winslow is already on the ground scratching the creature and making him purr.

Greer turns my way. "Lottie, Winslow and I are sorry we can't help you find Everett. But you do realize, lending a helping hand to humans is not within the guidelines."

"Don't worry about it. I just wish you had sonar or something. Can't you just think about him and land in his presence?"

She shakes her head. "We're about as useless as you are."

"Nice. In that case, I'll see you later."

"We'll see you at Honey Lake on Saturday!" Greer chimes.

I nod. "Beasty, I expect to see you soon enough to work on Jana's case."

I head back into the dining room where Noah and I say goodnight to Lainey and Meg and to my mother and Mayor Nash out front as well.

We make a beeline for Main Street and head straight for Mangias. We called in a large pepperoni pizza to take back to the house with us. The cashier is a man named Nico and he has our order ready as we walk in the door.

"Every night you two order the same thing." He laughs as he takes Noah's credit card and processes it. "You know, you're not alone. Every night I get a call for a large pepperoni—but for that one, I gotta drive myself all the way out to Hollyhock. Not fun. The gal is a good tipper, though." He hands Noah the receipt and I note the fact Noah is a good tipper, too.

We take off for Country Cottage Road, the cozy little street we live on.

When Noah and I were dating last fall, I found a rental across the street from his cabin. And coincidentally, Everett bought the house next door to mine. We've been one big dysfunctional family ever since.

Noah and I land on my sofa as Pancake and Waffles sit on either side of us like a couple of fluffy Himalayan pillows.

"Who's the first suspect, Lottie?"

"Why the boyfriend, of course." I lean in and bear hard into his evergreen eyes. "If I've learned anything, it's you can't trust a thing a boyfriend might tell you."

Noah lifts his brows and shoves another bite of pizza into his mouth.

You can't argue with the truth.

CHAPTER 5

The Cutie Pie Bakery and Cakery is filled to capacity with cake hungry customers. The Fourth of July is closing in on us and flags and patriotic buntings line almost all of Honey Hollow, but not one part of me feels like celebrating anything. The scent of fresh baked pink champagne cake permeates the air as Lily and I struggle to keep up with the crowd.

My mother just sent over an entire busload of

tourists who finished up with her haunted B&B tour for what she's dubbed as The Last Thing They Ate Tour. Yes, my mother actually pitches a nonexistent tour of my bakery just to help boost my sales at the expense of the latest homicide. And how I hate the fact one of my baked goods is somehow always at the center of attention at the scene of the crime. I truly do sell out of whatever baked good the deceased happened to be eating at the time of his or her demise.

Poor Jana.

There's been a run on my pink champagne cake like never before. And, believe you me, I've been sneaking a swig out of the bottle every now and again. I've made it a habit to leave the last inch for me. I would never dream of cross-contaminating my baked goods. But boy, did I need it to take the edge off.

I've got Everett's picture right on the front counter. A few of the tourists have asked if he's a celebrity that's come through town, so I had Lily print up a tiny banner that reads MISSING just above his forehead. It's eerie and frightening and makes this entire nightmare all too real.

Beasty prowls to and fro as I finish slicing up another pink champagne cake.

"How did you know Jana?" I whisper over to him as I move the cake to the front counter where Lily takes over.

Beasty belts out a rather unimpressive roar. "Her

father dealt in the illegal sale of exotic animals." He rolls his Rs and it's entirely adorable. "I was one of them. I resided with the March family for a total of three weeks before I was sold to a restaurateur with a penchant for the extravagant. Once he was apprehended by the Mounties, I was placed in a zoo in Montreal."

"Nice. International crime. Who would have known? Jana was a very nice girl. But just three weeks? She really fell hard for you."

"The tears the girl shed when we parted ways." He shakes his beautiful head. "I cried for her as well. She was my second mother."

"That's so heartbreakingly sweet."

Lily pokes her head back into the kitchen. "What's *sweet*, Lottie? Are you talking to yourself again?"

"The cake is sweet. Do we need more?"

"No, but your sister and her fiancé are here."

"Ooh!" I skip to the front, thrilled to find Lainey and Forest out front. "Let's take a seat." I scoop up a plate full of cookies and Forest's favorite dark fudge brownies as I meet them at the table. My ex Bear helped paint the interior of the bakery a delicious butter yellow. The furniture is hodgepodge, mismatched and painted in every shade of pastel. "Can I get you some coffee?"

Lainey shakes her head. "This is more than enough." She slides a bloated notebook my way. "Our realtor is meeting up with us here in just a few minutes. Here's the holy grail, Lottie. This was Jana's notes for my wedding.

You don't know how hard it is for me to part with the original."

"These are notes?" I marvel as I open the dictionary-sized three-ring binder with a picture of a wedding cake over the front. "I know you've got a lot on your plate, but do either of you have any idea of who would want to hurt Jana?"

Forest and Lainey exchange a glance, and I get the vaguest feeling they're holding something back.

Forest takes a breath. "Jana mentioned something about having a falling-out with Jackie."

"Jackie?" I think back to the convention. "The short girl with the wild black hair? That was her best friend, right? They seemed to get along fine for the five minutes I saw them."

Lainey shrugs. "And they did. But Jana said there was tension. She never specified what it was about, but maybe Jackie still wanted Jana's fiancé for herself? The guy is a looker."

Forest growls and Lainey leans in and gives the scruff on his cheek a scratch.

How I miss Everett's scruff. How I miss Everett's everything.

"*Aw.*" Lainey takes up my hand. "You're thinking about him again, aren't you?"

"Oh, I don't dare stop. I know Everett would do the same for me. He'd tear apart all of Vermont until he brought me home safe." My chest bucks as I do my best to control my emotions. "It's just so frustrating knowing he's out there somewhere and I can't do anything at all to find him."

Forest leans in. "Noah told me about the note at the convention."

Lainey sucks in a lungful of air so fast I'm afraid she might accidentally vacuum up all the cookies right off the platter. "What? You mean to tell me there were *two* maniacs running around the convention center that afternoon? That's it. This planet's not safe anymore. We're moving, Forest."

"To Mars?" I couldn't help but ask.

Before my sister can answer, a redhead with her hair pulled into a bun, a pink silk jacket, and matching skirt saunters over.

"You two ready to shake up Honey Hollow?"

Lainey snatches a peanut butter cookie off the plate. "Do they have a Honey Hollow on Mars?"

"Never mind her," I say. "I'm Lottie. I think we met briefly at the convention center. Hey, you were the girl Jana introduced us to. The event planner from Ashford?"

"That would be me. I just started my own event company—Make It Happen. I'm hoping it will take off soon. Hook is letting me take on these two because he's seen how desperately I need to make ends meet. The real estate market is a bit slow in these parts, and most realtors have other means to supplement their income."

"Makes sense." I slide the cookie platter her way. "Sweet treat for the road?"

"*Ohh*, thank you." She goes for the rocky road brownie, a tried-and-true favorite. "I remember you from the convention, too. So tragic what happened." She shudders. "I hope this doesn't sound callous, but I'm sure glad I know who her clients are. I mean, those people are going to need someone to step in and I'll gladly be that person for them. In memory of Jana, of course."

Huh. That sounds both callous and heroic. Something tells me it takes a talent to do just that.

The three of them take off, and I schlep the oversized notebook back to the counter with me.

Keelie bops over from next door as Lily finishes up with the last of the tourists.

"Whatcha got?" Keelie spins the folder her way. "Lemon-Donovan wedding. Wow, don't tell me this is the instruction manual. I promise when Bear and I get hitched, it won't be nearly as over organized. I'm thinking of keeping it simple. I bet I could pull the whole thing off in a month."

"Keelie! Are you trying to tell me that you and Bear are engaged?"

"What? No way. We're still in the puppy love stage, but a girl can dream."

"Or scheme," Lily snips before taking off again.

"So what's the deal with Mr. Sexy?"

Mr. Sexy happens to be the nickname baristas the world over have gifted Everett, and I don't disagree with their intuitive assessment.

"Still missing. Keelie, I'm going to go insane if I can't find him soon. I have to know he's safe. What if he's hurt? What if he needs medical attention? This person is a psychopath."

"Something has to give soon, Lottie. And I'm hoping whatever it is, it's good news."

"It has to be. We won't accept anything less."

"What about Jana's case? Anything new?"

My eyes flit to the door. "Amanda Wellington just climbed to the top of the suspect list. She admitted to having financial trouble and she seemed more than happy to take over Jana's clients."

"What about her fiancé? He is a looker."

"Funny. Lainey said the same thing. I guess compared to Everett and Noah, I didn't notice—no offense to Bear. I'll try to track him down. Maybe I'll find out where his office is and we can bring him some cookies?"

Keelie and I have made a habit of showing up at a suspect's place of work with a platter full of sweet treats. Let's just say it doesn't always yield such sweet results.

She makes a face. "From what I heard he has a home office."

"Then we'll go with plan B."

"What's plan B?"

"I have no idea, but B had better stand for *brilliant*."

Beasty treks over, his hulking frame lumbering as his shoulders fall and rise with every step. He's so gorgeous with his snow-white mane, pale gray stripes, and startling blue eyes.

"I sense a presence," he rumbles it out like a threat.

"A presence?" My antennae go up as I scan the vicinity.

Keelie squints over at me. "Did you say presents?"

"Yes! *Yes*, I did." I dash over to the door and look up and down the street. "It's a bright sunny day, almost eighty degrees out, and most of the tourists are taking cover in the air-conditioned shops."

Keelie pops up beside me. "Lottie, you just gave me a brilliant idea. We need to have a naughty nightie party for Lainey. It's the least we can do after your murderous Midas touch killed off her wedding planner."

My mouth falls open at the accusation, but before I can swat her, she's trilling out a string of things to do for the naughty party as she makes her way to the Honey Pot Diner next door.

At one point, our grandmother Nell Sawyer owned both the Honey Pot Diner and the bakery—and, well, half of Honey Hollow. When she died, she left the lion's share of it all to yours truly, due to the fact she felt so bad she needed to hide her familial connection to me in order to honor her daughter's request.

The Honey Pot Diner is connected to the bakery

through a walkway blown through our connecting wall. There's a large resin oak tree that spreads its twinkle light strewn branches all the way across the Honey Pot's ceiling and well into the café of my bakery as well. The effect is simply magical.

I'm about to press my nose to the glass door once again and nearly get it taken off as it swings open and in walks Felicity Gilbert.

"Felicity," I say. "Welcome to the Cutie Pie, where the baker is always waiting at the door to greet you."

She laughs as I press my hand to my chest from the close call.

"Or to get her nose rearranged. Sorry about that." Felicity is an adorable redhead with shaggy hair and a sprinkling of freckles over her face. "I'm just hopping in to pick up a couple of slices of that pink champagne cake everyone is talking about for Carlotta and me. Your mother really has been a godsend at the shop."

Felicity's mother was Carlotta's childhood best friend and took her in when she came back into town last January. Unfortunately, Felicity's mother was brutally murdered a few months back. And since then, Felicity has been navigating the flower business with the help of Carlotta.

"Well, I'm glad to hear she can be of help. How are you holding up? I know you and Jana were close."

"Very close. She was my college roommate and she

was my roommate right here in Honey Hollow. She and Pierce were house-hunting just before she passed."

"That's right. You lived together." House-hunting? "You wouldn't happen to know who their realtor was, would you? I mean, Lainey is looking for a house right now, too." Of course, they already have one, but I choose to omit that little detail.

"Amanda something or other."

"Amanda Wellington?"

"Yup. They were intermeshed in so many things. I think the pressure was mounting because they've been butting heads as of late. But before you get any funny ideas, Amanda didn't do this. She's not violent. I can no more imagine her firing a gun than I can you." She makes her way to the counter and Lily helps her out with a box of champagne cupcakes and a couple of iced lattes.

I have a gun. And I happened to have used it to defend myself against a killer just last month. But Felicity doesn't know that. It makes me wonder what she doesn't know about Amanda.

Felicity breezes by.

"Tell Carlotta I said hello!" I wave as she takes off for the flower shop.

Lily comes over and hands me a blank envelope. "Found this tucked in the back door."

"Huh, that's strange. There's nothing printed on the front." My heart drums in my chest as Beasty slinks over and stands at attention. His head is as high as my chest, he's that huge.

My fingers do their best to work it open and I pull out a single black heart. Written in white are the most frightening words of all—*It's over*.

CHAPTER 6

*T*here is no place more special than Honey Lake on the Fourth of July. The sun is setting and a pale wash lies over the water, shimmering as if it were liquid gold. The lake itself is seven miles long by two and a half miles at its widest. It sits nestled with brown sugar sand and evergreens, both of which add to its fairy-tale charm.

The thick scent of grilled burgers and hot dogs fills

the air, and the laughter of the people gathered, the squeal of the children makes it feel as if we're at one big family reunion.

Noah and I have stretched a quilt out onto the sand not far from Keelie and Bear. Lainey and Forest are behind us as are Meg and Hook. My mother is at the picnic tables with her friends, Becca—Keelie's mother, Carlotta, and my uncle William, who is currently suing to have his mother's will disputed. Nell Sawyer, my lovely grandmother (a surprise to me as of January), is the one that left me the entire Eastern Seaboard, plus the land under my bakery. If I just got the land in the settlement, I would have been thrilled. I'll be the first to admit, the rest is a bit much.

But the one person who is missing today is Everett, and how I hate the fact he's missing.

Noah took the note Lily found at the bakery the other day. He can't figure out heads or tail what it could possibly mean.

"Lottie!" my mother calls from the picnic table and waves wildly until she catches my attention. "Yoo-hoo!" She does her best to wave me over, and I groan as soon as I see the sight behind her. Mayor Nash and my new siblings are mingling in the crowd. Kelleth and Aspen look stunning in their long summer dresses—red, white, and blue themed, of course—and their hair is milky in this dim light. Finn stands behind them looking adorable as he chats up a few girls from Naomi's naughty book club. Mayor Nash makes a grab for my mother's waist as if he owns it, and I can't help but wrinkle my nose at the sight.

Noah takes up my hand and helps me to my feet. "Come on, Lot. You might as well get it over with."

"Fine. But if I'm going down, I'm taking you with me."

Noah chuckles as we head on over. The night is quickly descending on us, and soon enough we'll be treated to a fireworks spectacular.

Mom wraps an arm over Noah's shoulder as she looks to me. "Be nice, Lottie. Like it or not, these are your siblings," she grits the words through her teeth, trying her best not to move her lips.

I step over to Finn, aka the nice one, and he offers up an impromptu hug. "What's up, sis? Noah?" He clinks his beer bottle to the one in Noah's hand. "Hey, why don't you two come up to the lodge sometime? I'm one of the managers at the Sugar Bowl Resort. I'll set you two lovebirds up with the honeymoon suite."

"Sounds good to me!" a female voice chirps from behind as Cormack comes in for the attack. I've wondered where she's been all day.

Finn frowns over at her as she rattles on and on about her room service preferences.

Lainey pops up. "Did someone say honeymoon?"

"Finn works at the Sugar Bowl Resort. He said he could set Noah and me up with the honeymoon suite."

Noah leans out of Cormack's range. "We should take it, Lot. Heaven knows we need a vacation."

Lainey giggles. "That man is still striving to get in your pants. Hey? Do you think your brother would help set me up with a honeymoon deal?"

"Lainey, don't you have your honeymoon mapped out yet?"

"Not really. Mom offered to buy us a fourteen-day cruise as a gift, but not only can Forest not get that kind of time off, he gets seasick." She makes a face. "And I want my honey to shoot me over the moon, if you know what I mean—not have his head buried in the toilet."

"Go ahead and ask. It looks like Finn would pay to have someone interrupt Cormack's list of demands."

I glance back and spot a sparkling spray of light over by the woods, and sure enough I see Beasty striding this way with a little moppet of a spook riding on his back, Lea. I take a step in the direction and knock right into a body—Kelleth.

"Excuse me," I say, offering a meager smile. She's holding hands with a man who looks about her age, tan, dark hair, square jaw, and thick bushy brows.

"Where are you off to?" Kelleth steps in my path as if this were a showdown. "Are you looking for my father so you can splash your drink in his face? You do realize that little stunt has cut you out of the will for life."

A dull laugh lives and dies in my chest. "Listen, Kelleth. I have no interest in your father or any of the cash and prizes he might be willing to part with upon his untimely death. I'm doing just fine on my own. I don't need anyone else's money, and I certainly don't need anything Harry Nash can provide."

The man holding her hand bellows out a laugh. "A woman after my own heart." He thrusts his hand forward. "Steven Compton. I'm Kelleth's fiancé."

"Nice to meet you, Steven, I'm Lottie Lemon, Kelleth's unexpected half-sister. I own and operate the Cutie Pie Bakery and Cakery down the street. Pop in anytime you want for a sweet treat."

Kelleth's over glossed lips contort in all sorts of ridiculous directions as if I just propositioned her fiancé. And I guess if your mind is in the gutter, it sure sounded that way.

"So what do you do for a living?" My lips stretch into a short-lived smile his way just as Noah joins us along with Cormack.

"I work for Underwood Investments, but I've been with the company since the beginning. That baby is practically mine."

"Underwood Investments?" I ask as Noah and I exchange a glance. "I bet you know Pierce. It's such a tragedy what happened to his girlfriend."

He closes his eyes a moment. "The worst news ever. Poor guy is a wreck. I've been steering the ship just to give him a breather."

Noah steps in. "Noah Fox. Lottie's friend." Just

hearing the platonic tag hurts my heart. Noah is so much more than a friend, but sadly there's no name for that gray zone. "What do you think happened? That was a pretty brutal murder."

Steven lifts a brow and shrugs. "Random, I guess. I mean, who would want to see Jana dead? The woman was a saint."

Kelleth shudders. "I bet it was one of those crazed bridezillas. I heard that convention was crawling with them. And don't think for a minute that planning a wedding can't bring out the worst in someone. I should know. Steven has been a real whiner." She brays like a donkey—a trait I'm thrilled not to have inherited in any way, shape, or manner.

"Cute." Steven dots her lips with a kiss. "But Kelleth is the whiner." He gives a sly wink her way and I like him more by the minute. "Hey?" He looks to Noah and me. "If either of you has some money parked that you can't figure out what to do with, give me a call." He whips out a thick business card and hands one to each of us.

"Thank you. I think we will," I say as I shed a secret smile Noah's way.

Noah looks to Steven. "What kind of investments do you specialize in?"

"Colored diamonds, binary options in varying markets from coffee to currency."

Lainey comes up. "I've got my honeymoon all

settled!" she trills with delight before bearing hard into my eyes. "And so help me, if you find a body between here and there, I'll hang you by your toes myself."

Kelleth steps forward. "My fiancé and I are tying the knot in February. And you?"

Lainey's vocal cords go off like a tightly coiled spring that's just been released as she pulls Kelleth to the side as if they were long-lost sorority sisters. Steven waves our way before wisely heading off toward the refreshment table.

Meg and Hook bounce our way.

Hook nods in the direction Steven just took off in. "Did that dude just try to rope you into binary options?" He pinches his eyes shut a moment. "Steer clear, guys. That's not what I would call a solid investment."

Hook is a solid investment for my sister. As much as I didn't care for his younger brother, Hook is an outstanding guy—especially now that he's no longer tangled up in a quasi-threesome with my sister and bestie. Hook used to run Wall Street before he moved back to run the real estate empire his father left him.

I lean in. "Have you ever heard of Underwood Investments? That's the investment firm Jana March's fiancé owns and runs."

He ticks his head back a notch. "I have heard of Underwood Investments. It's a pretty big deal. They employ half of New York City. Sounds like I'll have to catch up with the guy and chew the financial fat."

"Here. Take this." I hand Hook the business card in my hand. "I'll share with Noah."

"Thanks." Hook slips it into his back pocket. "And if there's anything I can do to help bring Everett back, just let me know. I'll do whatever I can."

"Thank you. I appreciate that."

Noah and I take off for the boulders shrouded with evergreens where it's just a touch quieter and the ground is elevated enough to give us a bird's-eye view of the lake.

A spray of glittering stars seems to be moving near the waterline and I take a breath at the sight. That glorious tiger hops right out of the supernatural constellation and lands deftly at the base of the lake. The shadow of a little girl is seated on his back.

"Noah, I wish you could see this. Beasty just trotted to the lake and is trying to lap up the water. Little Lea is riding him like a pony, spanking his backside." I give a little laugh just as a couple of luminescent beings steal my attention. "And if I'm not mistaken, that's Greer and Winslow sitting at the water's edge."

"It sounds like every soul in Honey Hollow came out to see the fireworks."

"Every soul but Everett." My gaze locks on the ripples shimmering out from the center of the lake. "Noah, be honest with me. Do you think he's—you know, still alive?"

A warm breeze pushes my hair away from my face,

and if I didn't know better, I'd say it felt as if it just offered up a tender kiss to my lips.

"I do." Noah wraps his arms around me as he pulls me close. "And I'll tell you why. Everett finally admitted to loving someone other than himself—and that someone was you." He leans in and dots a kiss to my nose. "Sorry." His brows bounce with something just this side of regret. "And if I know Everett like I think I do, he's not going anywhere if he can help it. He's going to fight to get back to the best thing in the world, and that's you, Lottie." He tightens his grip for a moment. "I know I'd fight like hell to get back to you, Lot."

"You're very sweet." I bite down over my lip as I consider what Everett must be going through. "I'm thinking she has a gun."

"And maybe a cage. Honestly, I don't know what in the hell is going on."

"She could be drugging him."

The first flare shoots up into the navy sky and the entire lake glows pink as it explodes overhead in a spray of fiery glory.

"He's coming home to you, Lottie. I'm making sure of this myself."

"You?" I tease as I pull back to get a better look at him.

"Yes, me." Noah's dimples dig in deep and my stomach bisects with heat. I hate that they still have their power over me. "I'm doing it for you—and I'm doing it for him. I care about him. I always have and I always will. We were brothers for a season. And believe it or not, before things went south, there was a bond between us. Everett used to toss the ball around with Alex and me."

"You hardly ever talk about your brother."

He shrugs as the fireworks explode overhead once again, a purple umbrella that sprays over the sky and disappears with less than a whisper.

"He's younger by a year. Ex-Marine turned investment banker. He's in Florida with my mother. He said he might come out next month to visit with friends. And I hope he does. I'd love for you to meet him."

"Oh? Is he single?" I tease.

Noah pushes his shoulder to mine as the fireworks spectacular picks up steam. We watch in awe as the sky lights up like a neon rainbow, as fanciful fireworks create a pattern of wonder and beauty and leave us breathless and mesmerized. It goes on for what feels like a blissful eternity, and when the grand finale hits, I'm already a bit mournful that's its coming to an explosive conclusion.

The last burst detonates, followed by the quiet hush of smoke and the din of a faint applause.

Noah leans over and lands a kiss to my cheek. "Happy Fourth of July, Lottie. I'm glad I got to share it with you."

"I'm glad I got to share it with you, too."

"Maybe next year we'll have Everett back and he'll be the best man at our wedding." He helps me to my feet.

"Funny. But we're not getting near a wedding of our own as long as Cormack is wearing my ring."

A warm chuckle bounces through him. "She gave the ring back to me for safekeeping a few days after she took it. She had her jeweler make up a replica."

I suck in a quick breath. "And you let me keep thinking she snaked my ring!" I give his arm a playful pat.

He lifts a shoulder. "Maybe I wanted to see if you cared."

"Noah"—I reach up and give his scruff a scratch—"you know I care. You know I love you. And you also know we wouldn't be in this predicament if—"

He runs his finger softly over my lips. "I know. And it agonizes me to hear it."

I glance down at the water and a peculiar sight catches my eye. "Hey? Look at that," I say, pointing over to where my new brother has an arm around a familiar blonde bombshell—the official Mrs. Fox herself. "Maybe you'll be getting that divorce just in time for your birthday next month." My stomach squeezes tightly because honestly, that feels all too soon.

"Maybe I will." He pats my back. "I'm surprised you remembered my birthday."

"I remember everything about you, Noah Corbin Fox." I hike up onto my tiptoes and offer his cheek a kiss. "And as long as I have breath in my lungs and I highly suspect afterwards, I will never forget you. And speaking of not forgetting, how about we grab some Chinese in honor of Everett before we head home?"

"Sounds like a plan."

Noah and I call it in and run into the Wicked Wok to pick it up. The cashier runs Noah's credit card—Noah is far too stubborn to ever let me pay.

"Hey guys," he says, pulling up the receipt. "One order of Kung Pao chicken, one order of beef with broccoli, and two orders of cream cheese wontons."

I exchange a mournful glance to Noah. That was Everett's favorite and he always insisted we get two orders of those cream cheese wontons.

"Here you go." The cashier slides the bag our way. "Funny thing is, we've gotten this exact same order every single night for the last two weeks. I thought I was finally going to meet the mystery woman." He chuckles. "But it turns out, we already delivered that one—all the way out in Hollyhock."

"I guess it's a popular order," I muse.

We say goodnight to the young man and head back to my place.

And all night I wonder why it feels as if I've heard that same story about Hollyhock before.

CHAPTER 7

The Cutie Pie Bakery and Cakery is nearly cleaned out after a vigorous morning rush. It's almost eleven as another crop of customers head on in, this time with far more familiar faces.

Carlotta trots my way, and I spot Naomi Turner scuttling in after her wearing a tight pink dress and matching heels. There's a hot pink gift bag wagging in her hand as she makes her way to Lily.

"What's up, Lot?" Carlotta points to the coffee machine, and I get right to pouring her a cup. "Any news on that beefy boyfriend of yours?"

"Nope. The nutcase who has him has come by the bakery, though, so Noah is out back having a security system installed that will cover this place from every angle."

"Wow. Do you think they're coming after you next?"

"I doubt it. Whoever she is seems quite content to keep things status quo."

Keelie bops over along with Lily and Naomi.

Keelie lands an arm around my shoulders. "Still no word, huh?"

"Nope. Contrary to unpopular opinion, Everett is being held against his will." I take a moment to glare at Naomi.

Lily huffs, "I bet he ticked off someone in his courtroom. Rumor has it, he was just as hard on people in the courtroom as he was in the bedroom."

I don't bother teasing apart that double entendre.

Naomi swoons as if she were trying to envision it. "Hopefully, he'll be back before Lainey's wedding. I was looking forward to cutting in on a slow dance with him."

I make a face her way. "Yes, well, once Everett comes home, his dance card will be completely filled, by *me*."

She lifts a sassy shoulder my way. "I guess I'm free to dance with Detective Fox then."

My mouth falls open. "His dance card is all filled up, too."

"Knew it!" Naomi bucks with a laugh. "You want them both for yourself. Admit it, Lottie. You have some twisted thing happening among the three of you. I just knew something tragic would come out of it."

Lily tips her head my way. "Hey? Maybe Detective Fox should be investigated."

Carlotta honks out a laugh. "No way, no how."

"Thank you," I say. "It's about time someone comes to Noah's defense."

Carlotta inches back. "I wasn't coming to his defense. I'm saying why bother? They won't catch him. My money says that boy pumped the good judge full of bullets and buried him in the desert."

"There's not a desert for a thousand miles," I'm quick to say. "And Noah hasn't left my sight."

Lily gargles out a laugh. "That's because he's sleeping in your bed, Lottie."

"My couch," I correct just as a familiar group of women stream on in. It's all the usual suspects from Naomi's naughty book club, or heck, it might even be a get-together for her new endeavor, the Homicide in Honey Hollow Club. Although each of the women filing in and taking a seat in the café happens to have a tiny little gift bag attached to her wrist. "Hey? What's going on? Are we celebrating someone's birthday?" I do a quick mental check of the cakes I have in back.

"Nope." Lily pulls her own little gift bag out from below the counter. "Not a birthday. In fact, you might just say it's Forest Donovan's lucky day."

I'm about to dig a little deeper when Meg and Lainey burst in through the door. Meg has a dozen hot pink balloons attached to her hand.

"Here she is!" Meg blows a party horn and scares away what little real customers I had left in the bakery. "The woman of the hour!" She pops a rhinestone-encrusted tiara on Lainey and navigates her to the center of the room as the girls all break out into cheers.

"What is going on?" I'm both mildly alarmed and amused.

Naomi flicks her glossy dark hair off her shoulder. "Nothing that concerns a prude like you."

"I'm not a prude. I've slept with two men in the last year alone. I believe that's the opposite of a prude." A fact I'm not too proud of.

Naomi chortles to herself. "I believe the word you're looking for is *skank*, Lottie."

Keelie pulls two glossy red bags from behind her back and waves them in the air. "It's Lainey's naughty nightie party!"

A heavy groan comes from me as three customers who just walked in turn right around and head back out onto Main Street.

"Great. And there go my afternoon profits." I get right to the tasks of pulling out my freshest pink champagne cake and slicing it up for Lainey's naughty guests. "If we can't beat 'em, we might as well join 'em." I wink over to Carlotta as I hand her the first slice.

Lily starts to distribute the dessert just as my mother and Mayor Nash breeze through the door.

"Lottie Lemon!" Mayor Nash flashes that politician smile—most likely the same one he gave Carlotta right before I was conceived. A married man and a *sixteen-year-old*. Just the thought makes me want to pop him in the nose. What was he thinking all those years ago?

Carlotta scoots next to me. "What am I? Chopped liver?"

"Carlotta." Mayor Nash nods her way. "It's a pleasure as usual."

"I bet it was a pleasure," I mutter below my breath and my mother shoots me a look that could pull the screws right out of the wall.

The crowd in the café breaks out into catcalls as Lainey holds up a black sexy number with far too many straps and far too few pieces of fabric.

Mom sucks in a breath. "The naughty hottie party! Was that today?"

"Yuppers." I can't help but manufacture a smile at the man who had a hand among other parts in making me. "Unfortunately, it's women only, so you might be uncomfortable if you hang around any longer. We will totally understand if you feel the need to leave. Like right now."

Carlotta howls with a laugh. "Honey, this man has seen more naughty nighties than the Scarlet Sage Boutique stocks in the back!"

Mayor Nash grins as he silently affirms this naughty theory.

Mom clicks her tongue his way. "I'm sorry, Harry. I have to stay. You'll have to go on to the council meeting without me."

"Council meeting?" I'm pretty sure my mother has done more than her fair share of civic duty as of late. And hanging out with Mayor Nash is really pushing the envelope.

"Yes"—she frowns his way—"Harry was going to introduce me to the board and I was going to try to get my horticulture club approved to work on the grounds around the fountain in Town Square. I thought we could spruce it up in time for fall."

Mayor Nash leans in her way. "You know who's *falling*? Me." He gives a cheesy wink before dotting a kiss to her lip. "Ladies." He tips his head our way before his eyes settle on mine. "Lottie, if you don't mind, I'd love to come in sometime and just spend a little time with you. Maybe we can go to dinner one night?"

"Maybe," I say as he waves and takes off. And by maybe, I meant no.

Mom makes her way to the hot bed of insanity as Lainey pulls a silver lace number out of a bag and it shines and shimmers just like something you'd see at

Red Satin. For whatever reason, that makes me miss Everett all the more.

Lord knows Everett and I logged some serious time at the Red Satin Gentlemen's Club while tracking down our fair share of killers. And now Jana March's killer gets to roam free as does that maniac who's holding Everett hostage. It's clear my crime-solving mojo has been stunted without my favorite judge by my side spurring me along.

Carlotta yanks me over to the party right along with her. "I can't believe your mother is still interested in that glorified gigolo."

"You and me both. I don't like it. In fact, I charge you with the task of finding her a new man. Drum one up, call one back from the dead—except the last one. He was sort of a dud himself." No joke. Mom's old boyfriend was just this side of psychotic.

Lainey opens gift after naughty gift, and to my surprise she opens a hot pink number that's from me.

Keelie gives my shoulders a squeeze. "I took care of you, Lot. I figured you have enough on your plate, what with looking for the killer—trying to track down Everett and tend to all the details of Lainey's wedding."

Lainey pauses to look my way. "Don't forget the final payments are all due this week. I left the checks in an envelope in your folder." She narrows her eyes with a scrupulous stare. "And I bet you haven't even cracked your planner yet."

Good Lord! I can't even remember where I put that bloated book. Gah! I cannot ruin Lainey's wedding on top of botching up almost everything else.

Lainey goes on to open the rest of her raunchy gifts, and just as she gets to the very last one, Forest strolls in brandishing two dozen long-stem roses for his true love and the entire room breaks out into a choir of coos.

Bodies stand all at once as Meg and I help clean up the colored tissue tornado.

Meg hisses my way, "Did you see that list we need to tackle?"

"I…uh…"

"Ha!" Meg honks a laugh. "It looks like Lainey had the wrong sister pegged. So who's on your suspect list, Lot? Let's nail that killer so you can get your head back in the game."

"Only if the game is finding Everett."

Noah walks in and spots Lainey holding up a naughty nightie and he winces at the sight.

"Ladies." Noah lands before Meg and me. "I've got news, Lottie."

"Great. Is the bakery officially security central? I feel safer already."

"Yes," he muses. "But that's not the big news. I just got an alert from the bank. Someone tried making a very large wire transfer from Everett's bank account to the Bank of Hollyhock."

"What? Oh my goodness. We've got them. Who was it? Where can we find Everett?"

Noah blows out a slow breath. "I wish it was that easy. I had his bank accounts frozen, so the transaction was rejected. There's no way to know who would have been on the receiving end of it."

"Hollyhock." I look to Meg and shake my head.

"What is it, Lot?" She gives my shoulder a rattle as if shaking the answer right out of me.

"I don't know. It just seems to be a reoccurring theme. I mean, the odds are good this person who has him lives in Hollyhock if they bank there. Is there any way to get a list of their clients?"

Noah shakes his head. "That information is confidential."

"Hollyhock..." The name spins through my mind like a haunting song. "Wait a minute." My heart drums wildly. "Noah? Wasn't it strange that both the guy from Mangias and the guy from Wicked Wok said they had similar orders they delivered to Hollyhock? Isn't that a little out of range for them? I mean, it's almost as if—"

"Everett's communicating with us."

Noah and I bolt out the door and we don't stop until we get to Mangias.

CHAPTER 8

*J*uly is the only month of the year that the weather seems to be consistently, well—hellish. Our sweet small town has effectively been transformed into a toaster oven for all practical purposes.

By the time Noah and I cross the street, a mere one hundred yards, I'm sweating as if I just ran the Ashford

Marathon. My hair clings to the back of my neck, I'm panting up a storm, and Noah is giving me that bedroom eye as if he likes what he sees.

Noah opens the door to Mangias and the cool air greets us, right along with the heavenly scent of a fresh baked pizza. An entire thicket of people waits to be seated, each fanning themselves after narrowly escaping the flames from the sun. Come to think of it, it is lunchtime. But my appetite has taken a leave of absence, and all I can think about is finding my way to Everett.

Before I can accost the cashier, I spot an all too familiar shimmering aura of light coming from the dining room, and sure enough a gorgeous creature of ghostly proportions slinks his way over.

I take up Noah's hand. "Beasty is here," I whisper.

"Lottie," Beasty roars out my name low and dramatic, the exact way Everett was prone to do during our most heated moments—albeit my surname—and I feel terrible for reliving the memory. "You're just in time to have an impromptu run-in with someone very special to my sweet Jana."

I think it's adorable the way he referenced her as his *sweet Jana*.

Noah takes a look around at the crowd in the reception area. "They look locked up. A stroll through the dining room couldn't hurt."

"Let's do it."

Beasty leads the way and both Noah and I straighten when we see him.

Pierce Underwood sits at an intimate table for two with a brunette who has her back to us. Her hand stretches across the table to grab ahold of his, but he quickly withdraws his fingers.

Huh.

Noah and I casually stroll by before I backtrack.

"Pierce?" I ask, perhaps a little too cheery.

Both Pierce and his companion look our way and it's only when I see her face I recognize her as well.

"Oh, and you're…" I'm at a loss for Jana's best friend's name. Beasty growls as he hops up onto the table and it's a menacing sight.

"Jackie." She presses her black fingernails to her chest. "You're the baker, right? From the convention?"

"Yes. And unfortunately, my sister's new wedding planner." I offer a mournful smile to both of them. "I'm so sorry about everything you're going through."

"Thank you." Pierce nods as he looks to Noah. "Detective Fox. How's the investigation?"

Noah's dimples press in as he glances my way. "I interviewed Pierce at the scene." He looks back his way. "I wish I had better news. Whoever did this must have lured her out back and out of range of any security cameras the convention center had set up."

Jackie shudders. "I don't know who did this to her,

but when I get my hands on that person—and I will—they're a goner." She twists her body to get a better look at Noah. "No offense, detective, but I'm going to save you a heck of a lot of trouble and the taxpayers a heck of a lot of money. That person is just as dead as Jana."

That was convincing—even if she does turn out to be the killer.

Beasty grunts and the table quivers, but no one seems to notice.

Pierce takes a breath as he looks my way. "Wait a minute. You're the baker that Felicity says brought down her mother's killer?"

A breath hitches in my throat. How I hate that my reputation precedes me. It really does ruin a lot of good sleuthing opportunities. As for example…

"That would be me." I dip my knees a bit as if the thought humbled me—more like enraged. "That was just a lucky shot, though. Right place, wrong time. Total fluke. Wouldn't you say?" I slap Noah on the back and accidentally give his gun a whack.

"Geez." Noah coughs as he maneuvers his way out of his own line of fire. "Yes, Lottie just had a stroke of luck." He looks to Pierce. "So, is there anything we can do for you?"

"Oh yes," I'm quick to interject. "Of course, I'll bake cookies for the funeral."

Jackie nods. "That's very kind. It will be small. Her mother passed away years ago and her father is in

Europe doing who knows what. She hasn't talked to him in months and I have no way of getting in touch with him either. It will just be her friends from town and a few from college. Sad in a way. Jana was such a great person. I wish the whole world could have seen how bright her light was."

There she goes again. Something about the way she's talking Jana up doesn't sit well with me. Although in all fairness, Jana was a bright light in an ever-dimming world.

"It sounds like you just adored her," I say.

"Oh, I did," Jackie nods frenetically. "In fact, the three of us were very close—not Pierce." She giggles nervously as she looks his way. "His sister Tracy. She teaches ballroom dance. That's initially why I had Jana meet her—you know, building up a connection for her new business, but I also knew that Pierce would be at his sister's studio that day and the rest as they say was fate." She takes a breath as she loses her gaze to some far-off place.

I offer a peaceable smile. "It sounds like your matchmaking skills were spot-on." My teeth graze over my lips for a moment. Tracy—Underwood maybe? Whatever her last name is, she's the next person on my list. "Oh, Tracy?" I rock back on my heels. "Doesn't she have that dance studio out in Fallbrook?"

"Leeds," Pierce is quick to correct as if Leeds were the better of the two.

Of course, it's in Leeds. Leeds is a cesspool of "dance"

studios. Why do I get the feeling the ballroom thing is just a clever front for the moves she's really teaching on the sly?

Noah scratches his chin. "Underwood Ballroom?"

"That's the one." Pierce beams with brotherly pride, and I note the slight dimple in his chin. Hey? Didn't my mother once tell me not to trust a man with a dimple in his chin? It's silly, I know, but my subconscious secretly drinks down whatever advice Miranda Lemon slings my way.

I shoot Noah a look that says *good work, detective.* It looks like Noah and I make a good crime-fighting duo, after all.

Their food arrives and I give a quick wave. "Well, I guess we'll see you at the funeral. If you can think of anything else you need, I'll be right across the street. I hope you're both taking time off work to try to cope with everything you're going through."

"Oh, we are." Jackie unfurls her napkin and sets it on her lap. "I'm taking off this week and next. I'll be back shortly after the funeral, but Pierce is leaving town."

Pierce rolls his eyes at Noah. "I'm not leaving town, detective." He gives a disapproving yet playful look to Jackie. "Way to make me sound guilty. A buddy of mine has a yacht in Greece. He invited me to head over and we'll take a nice long trip. I plan on sleeping the entire time. I just can't imagine my life without her." His voice breaks. "I'm sorry."

We wrap it up and say a quick goodbye as Beasty follows us to the front.

"What did you think?" he roars it out with a masculine appeal.

"I don't know," I whisper. "But it looks like the detective and I are about to trip the lights fantastic."

Noah's chest rumbles with a dark laugh as we head to the front to find the waiting area cleared out.

He leans in. "Let me handle this, Lot."

Nico, the manager, greets us. He's tall, sinewy, and looks freshly scrubbed with milky white teeth and a winning smile to show them off. "Noah, Lottie, table for two?"

"Actually..." Noah flashes his badge. "I'm here on official business. I hear you have a delivery made each day to Hollyhock. Is that right?"

Nico inches back and stares at Noah's badge as if it were the barrel of his gun.

"That's right. It happens. Last I checked that wasn't against the law, right?" He gives a nervous laugh.

"Nope." Noah chuckles right back as he puts his badge away and already Nico seems to be breathing easier. "It's just not your regular delivery range, is it?"

"We do it now and again. This one's pretty close to town, so it's not a big deal. Good tipper, too."

"I see. Nico, I'm going to be honest with you. I need the address of where you're making that delivery."

He lifts his hand and that nervous laugh comes right

back. "I'm afraid that's not going to happen. We reserve the right to keep our customers' privacy *private*. It's simply against company policy for me to share that information with you." His brows pinch as if he were suddenly angry. "And don't go following my delivery guys either. We don't want any trouble. If this person turns out to be a nutcase, I don't want them coming back and blowing a hole through my front windows."

"Not a problem." Noah pats the reception counter. "Have a great rest of the day, Nico."

I say an abrupt goodbye as Noah and I head out into the over bright day.

Beasty bounces right through the wall as if it were a hoop at the circus.

"That went well," I say as we head over to the canopy, hungry for a foot of shade. "Beasty, can you follow that driver?"

He lets out a furious roar. "I'm only able to appear where I'm needed, or within the realm of your presence. I'm sorry, Lottie. Lea and I have already tried."

"Shoot. I'm so frustrated I could blow a hole through Nico's window myself."

"You don't have to." Noah nods down the street. "We haven't hit Wicked Wok yet."

Noah, Beasty, and I hustle our way over and this time I do the talking, sweet and sugarcoated just like one of my snickerdoodle cookies that sells out before they ever get a chance to cool.

The young girl at the counter stops chewing her gum long enough to process what I'm saying. She has her hair in a messy bun and a pair of earbuds dangling from her neck.

"So you think that your boyfriend is cheating on you with some girl out in Hollyhock and you want to know her name?" Her mouth hangs open at the thought of my slightly unbelievable story.

"That's right. I just want to confront him, you know? Just tell him, I know you're having Kung Pao chicken, beef with broccoli, and two orders of cream cheese wontons with so and so."

A woodpecker-like laugh bubbles from her. "Hey, you really know their order."

"You bet I do." I feign the look of sudden grief. "It was once our order, too." True as gospel. And in all reality, I didn't have to fake an ounce of grief.

She narrows her gaze at Noah as if she were suddenly filled with suspicion. Heaven knows what she would think if she could see Beasty. Thank goodness for poltergeist-based mercies.

"Who's this guy?"

"Oh, he's—my brother."

Brother?

Heck, even the look on Noah's face echoes the sentiment.

"Oh, I see." She averts her eyes. "Yeah, my brother would totally tag along. He'd probably tear the guy from limb to limb, too." She flips the page on the weekly calendar in front of her and runs her finger down the page until it stops. "Hailey."

"Hailey." I elongate her name as I nod to Noah.

"Knew it." He scoffs, playing along brilliantly. "She's still on Willow, right?" He looks to the girl nonchalantly.

"Nope. Pine Brook."

I lean in and she slams the calendar shut.

"Sorry." She shrugs. "It's against our policy to give out addresses."

"Oh, I don't need it." I wrinkle my nose because I totally do. "I know exactly where Hailey lives. She thinks she's everything because she has such a nice place." I shudder.

"Right." The girl rolls her eyes. "Nice if you're a woodland creature."

A small crowd comes in and the girl gets right to seating them.

Noah and I hustle back out into the sizzling day.

"Hailey? That has to be her name," I say pleadingly as if demanding he confirm my theory.

"Maybe. How about this? I'll hang out in front of the bakery in my truck, and when I see them ready to leave I'll tail 'em."

"Not without me."

Beasty hops out of the front window and I take up Noah's hand.

Beasty lets out a gurgle of a roar. "She buried the

calendar under the register as soon as she got back. Sorry."

"Don't be. We'll be making that delivery right along with them. Come with us. We might need your help."

"Consider it done. But first, I need to swing by the bed and breakfast and pick up Lea. She's insistent on aiding in the effort." That promise I made her suddenly feels as if it's about to bite me in the behind—or more to the point, Greer's and Winslow's behind.

Beasty lets out an ear-splitting roar as he disintegrates before my very eyes—and no matter how many times I witness the unnatural event, I can never get used to it.

Noah looks up from his phone. "I just did a rough and dirty search of Pine Brook and it's a major backroad, lots of secluded cabins."

"Sounds like the perfect place to take an unwilling victim. Noah, I will scour each and every one of those hovels myself if I have to."

His lime green eyes meet with mine. "Not if I do it first."

"Everett's coming home, isn't he?" The words tumble out of me with a sigh.

"He's coming home, Lottie. I can promise you that."

A flood of relief hits me.

I can always count on Noah's word—with the exception of when he's tap-dancing around the truth.

And please, dear Lord, don't let that be now.

"To Hollyhock," I say as we head back down Main Street.

I just pray this doesn't lead to a dead end.

Or heaven forbid—a dead judge.

CHAPTER 9

*J*t turns out, Jana March was meticulous right down to the most intricate detail.

"Sweet Lord in heaven," I muse as I thumb through page after page of Jana's tome, which she affectionately referred to as her *wedding bible* as per the info printed on the very first page.

Noah and I are seated in front of the bakery while we wait for action down the street. It's almost four in the afternoon and the sun has finally stopped sending its hostile death rays over Noah's windshield.

I suggested we try to fry an egg on the hood of his truck, but Noah shot that brilliant idea down rather quickly, something about ruining his clear coat.

A choking sound emits from my throat. "How am I ever going to run through this list in the time I've got left? Lainey will be celebrating her silver anniversary before I finish half these things. When I get married, I'll be sure to chuck this bad boy and fly by the seat of my pants. It can't be that hard. I'll reserve the church, have the reception in my mother's conservatory, pick up a decent white dress from Scarlet Sage, and I'll bake my own cake, of course."

"Tell me when and where. I'll play the part of the groom." He picks up a tiny pair of binoculars and looks in the direction of the Wicked Wok.

I glance down at the ring on my finger. The one that belongs to Everett's mother. I'm far too paranoid to leave it at home, and when I'm at the bakery I put it in the ground safe in my office in a silver box that also houses a replacement part to my Hobart mixer. And oddly, every time I take it off, my finger feels naked, as if it were meant to house a serious piece of jewelry all along. I think a part of me wants this more than I know.

Beasty and Lea have spent the afternoon trotting up and down Main Street, with Lea riding him like a pony. They really are the cutest pair. I can't fathom why either of them doesn't want to return to paradise anytime soon, but if they do help me get Everett back, I have no idea how I'm going to keep my word to them. It was one of those things you agree to in a fit of delirium. And Everett missing has definitely sponsored a fit of delirium.

"And we're off." Noah puts the truck in gear. He's had the truck on the entire time shooting the AC at us or we would have melted by now. No sooner do the wheels start to move than a flash of lightning appears as Beasty and Lea materialize magically in the bed of the truck.

My heart starts racing, my adrenaline hits its zenith, and we haven't even left Honey Hollow yet.

"So this girl, Hailey"—Noah starts as he does his best to keep a decent distance from the delivery vehicle—"have you ever heard Everett mention her before?"

"No. In fact, the only other woman he's ever brought up was Harlow James—the one who was pregnant with his child and slid off the road and killed them both. Everett said she was nothing more than a one-night stand. He hardly knew the girl, but he was determined to raise his child."

"That's because he's a good guy."

My heart warms just hearing Noah say it. "That's quite an endorsement, considering you can't stand him."

Noah's dimples dig in and out. "Yeah, well. I've had a lot of time to think. I let my pride and jealousy get in the way of my relationship with Everett one too many times. Don't get me wrong—the thought of you two together kills me, but he's still family. He'll always be family."

"We'll always be family, too, Noah." There's an ache in my chest as I push the words out.

"We will, Lottie. And if I'm right, we'll be husband and wife one day, too."

We drive another ten minutes and follow the silver hatchback as it makes two stops right here in town before getting on the thoroughfare that leads to Hollyhock. We bypass the tract houses, the shopping mall, and any forms of quasi-city life as we head up the backroad toward Pine Brook Road.

The evergreens close in on us, darkening the skyline with their lofty limbs. Every now and again a cabin pops up between the thickets of pine trees. They're tiny, and adorable, and look as if they're made entirely out of Lincoln Logs.

"Oh my goodness, Noah, this is it!"

"Let's hope so." He hands me my phone. "I want you to text Ivy. Tell her I want her to monitor my vehicle until I contact her again."

"Does Ivy have a tracking device on your truck?"

"We both do. I've got one on yours, too. I'm thinking of adding Everett to the mix."

I know for a fact Noah put one on my mother's car and I'm thankful for it. That was back when she had a borderline psychotic boyfriend who needed to know her every move. Honestly, we all thought he was going to steal her away to some abandoned cabin and we'd never see her again. And here it was Everett we had to worry about the entire time. I put the text in to Ivy and she messages back with a thumbs-up. As much as I don't care for Ivy, she sure as heck just gave me a world full of comfort.

"They're slowing down," Noah whispers as he pulls off the side of the road and tucks us against an embankment lined with young pines.

"His car is going up that dirt road. Noah, we're going to lose him."

"No, we're not." He pulls out his binoculars and bites down over his lower lip as he inspects the road ahead. "Pine Brook Road number fourteen." He puts the car in reverse and starts to turn around.

"Noah, stop. What are you doing? The cabin is the other way. We have to go get Everett."

"Lottie, we can't just knock on the door and expect her to open it. We need to get a search warrant. I'm coming back with the deputies." There's a mournful tone in his voice. "Lottie, I'm sorry. I don't know what we're up against. I'm not putting you in that kind of danger."

Beasty and Lea pop their heads in from the back before forming fully in the back seat of the truck and I take up Noah's hand so he'll be apprised of whatever they might say.

Beasty growls as if he were as frustrated as I was. "Assign me a duty."

"Me, too," Lea snips. "I'm bored and you don't want to know what I'm capable of when I've been left to my own devices."

"Oh yes, I do. Beasty, you take Lea and go up the road to number fourteen. Go in that cabin and do a thorough search. And as soon as you find Everett, come right back down."

Noah's jaw redefines itself as he studies the road up ahead for signs of the silver hatchback.

"You both have less than twenty seconds, and then I'm turning this car around. The last thing I want is to arouse suspicion."

Beasty and Lea won't be stranded in the traditional sense, but they'll disappear from the area as long as I'm not in it.

In a flash of light that can rival a nuclear blast, Beasty and Lea bullet down the road and up the dirt driveway leading to the cabin just out of sight.

My body begins to tremble, and my breathing becomes erratic.

"Hey"—Noah wraps his arms around me tightly, warming my back with his hands—"you're shivering."

"I'm not cold. I'm just..." My teeth begin to chatter, disputing my claim.

"You're in shock, Lottie. You have both fight and flight working against each other." He pulls back, his sad eyes grazing over each of mine. "I love you, Lottie Lemon. And there's no way in hell I'd risk anything happening to you. This is as far as I come." He shakes his head. "I'm sorry."

Before I can berate him, or scream, or pull my hair out properly, Beasty and Lea appear in the back of the truck and I take up Noah's hand again.

"We saw nothing," Beasty growls it out in a fit of frustration as Noah backs up out and spins us in the opposite direction in a flash.

"What do you mean you saw nothing?" I peg Lea with a look as she glowers out the window as if she were planning a mass slaughter of the entire neighborhood.

"We could go to the door and no farther," she grouses. "We need you, Lottie. This cabin, these people have nothing to do with the murder Beasty came to help solve. And I've been forbidden entry as well."

"You're a ghost, Lea. Who is possibly going to stop you?"

"There are rules," Beasty rolls the R in *rules* dramatically.

"Well, I don't like the rules. Not in your world or in mine."

I hope Noah can read between the lines. If he doesn't think I'm coming back here, he obviously doesn't know me very well. I've got a gun—one *he* bought me. And I've got a couple of poltergeists who can do a heck of a lot of my dirty work for me if I can just get close enough to make the magic happen.

Noah takes us back to my place and he starts in on a search of property taxes to see who owns the cabin. A name pops up on the screen, and it takes a second for my mind to put two and two together.

"Oh my word, Noah," I say as we stare at the name on the screen. "You don't think... I mean, it can't be."

"I don't know, Lottie. But it sure as hell is one big coincidence if it's not."

"I don't believe in coincidences anymore, Noah."

"Good," he says, pulling his laptop forward and running a whole new search. "Because neither do I."

CHAPTER 10

The cabin on Pine Brook Road is owned by a man named Isaac James.

"Isaac James. *Hailey James.*" I look to Noah as we sit across from one another on my sofa. Pancake and Waffles fill the gap between us, the four of us snuggling as if we were one big happy family. The warm scent of vanilla permeates the air from the chocolate chip cookies I baked for Noah as soon as we walked through the door—his personal Kryptonite—and if it weren't for all the chaos in our lives at the moment, this would be bliss. I couldn't help the baking part. It's the only thing I know to do when I'm stressed to the max.

"Hailey James." He nods. "Harlow James."

The sun is cresting the horizon outside the window as the light in the room grows increasingly dim.

"You're not implying they're the same person, are you?"

"I don't know"—he says as his fingers dance over the keyboard of his laptop once again—"but I'm about to find out."

Noah hits the search engines hard, and sure enough pictures and articles begin to populate the screen.

"They're all about Harlow," I say, mesmerized by them all. "No mention of a Hailey. She could be a sister, a cousin, or an aunt."

"She could be Harlow."

"I guess you're right." My heart seizes at the bizarre thought. "At this point, anything is possible."

"Okay." Noah sets his laptop back on the coffee table. "I'm going to put in a call to Ivy. We'll try to get an emergency search warrant."

"Search warrant? Noah, we don't have time for that. We have to go now. If Everett is in there, he could be in grave danger. We've waited too long already." My voice hikes without my permission. "What has to happen in order to get a search warrant?"

"I have to meet with a judge and present probable cause."

"Meet with a judge? Like tonight?"

"Most likely in the morning."

"But Everett is in danger."

"We don't even know if he's in there."

"Well, I have probable cause to believe he is." I try to get up and Noah gently pulls me back down by the elbow.

"Lottie, I'm sorry, but the fact someone in Hollyhock likes pizza and Chinese food may not fly with the judge."

"What about the last name? It's the last name of the woman who died. She was the mother of his child. And the stalker last month? And the roses and the note?"

"Yes, but James is a common last name, and we're connecting an awful lot of dots. At best, I might be allowed to head over with a cruiser and ask the resident a few questions. It still may very well lead to Everett."

I glare at Noah for a good long while. While I can appreciate his need to submit to procedural orders, I am not amused at how reckless he's being with Everett's well-being.

"Darn right, it will lead to Everett," I say, bolting up in the other direction and making a beeline for my bedroom. I pick up the small Glock Noah and Everett bought me a couple months ago and shove it into my purse as I head for the door.

"Lottie, wait." Noah barricades the exit with this

body. "You cannot run off half-cocked. It's dangerous. You can get yourself killed."

Both Pancake and Waffles crane their necks over the arm of the sofa as if they were watching the show.

I close my eyes for a moment. "Beasty," I growl, and just like that, a spray of iridescent light fills my living room as the gentle oversized cat takes shape. "I'm headed to the cabin. Grab Lea and meet me there." The aura of a light goes out as efficiently as turning off a switch and my eyes meet with Noah's once again. "Step back. I have a gun and I am going to use it—several times this evening if need be."

"Lottie, I work for the Ashford Sheriff's Department. I can't go breaking the law. And I highly recommend you don't shoot me."

I tip my head to the side as I suck my lips in hard to keep from crying.

"If I were missing and you thought it was me up in that cabin"—my chest bucks with emotion—"would you follow procedure? Would you let *hours* pass? Would you have turned the truck around this afternoon?"

"This is different. Everett is built like a football player. He's strong."

"Not if he's dead." I shove Noah out of the way and bolt for my car.

"Lottie, wait!" he riots as he hurdles over the hood of my car and slides down in front of me. His chest palpitates wildly with his panting. His serious eyes bear hard into mine. "We'll take my truck."

A pang of guilt hits me as wide as the sea. "Noah, you can't risk your career."

"I can risk anything I want for you—and for Everett." His left dimple digs in deep as he ticks his head to the street. "Let's do this."

And we do.

A THOUSAND THOUGHTS sail through my mind on our way to Hollyhock.

What if I end up getting killed?

What if Noah gets killed?

What if Everett truly is already dead?

Should I text my mother and tell her I love her?

Send a group text to my mother and sisters?

Preemptively bequeath the bakery to Keelie?

And my cats! My sweet, precious cats. They can't lose me. Waffles already lost Nell. After all, it was Nell who bequeathed Waffles to me. Nell who was here haunting Honey Hollow just last month—who happened to have a very ominous warning about Everett's future—something about a casket and an altered future. Wait. Or was it Carlotta who mentioned the casket?

"Dear Lord, I can't think straight," I bleat as Noah gets off the highway and we head straight for Pine Brook Road.

"Lottie, you're going to have your weapon drawn. You will most certainly be thinking straight. Collect yourself. Take a deep breath. Remember, it's imperative to stay calm for Everett's sake."

"You're right." I take in a quick breath and nearly pass out. "So, what's the plan?"

"The plan is we park down the road, sneak up on the cabin, and search for signs of life. You'll stay five feet behind me at all times."

"That means you head into danger first. This doesn't please me, Noah."

"This isn't about pleasing you. It's about keeping you safe."

"And what about you?" I ask as I take in the ever-darkening woods around us.

"I'll be just fine." Noah kills the lights as we come upon the dirt driveway. He snuggles the truck up against an overgrowth of young pines, a little farther up than we were earlier today. "There's enough moonlight on the trail to our right. We should be fine."

The trail lights up like noonday as ethereal sparks begin to bloom, and Beasty appears with an enthusiastic Lea waving over at me.

"It turns out, I won't need a flashlight or the moon.

Beasty has lit up the trail like a beacon." I glance back to find Noah pecking manically into his phone.

"What are you doing?"

"Being very vague with Ivy in the event we run into trouble." He slips his phone deep into his pocket. "Get your gun, Lottie. And hold on tight."

I do as I'm instructed as we get out of the truck.

The air is warm as a gentle breeze licks by. The scent of damp earth and pine needles infiltrates the air. Noah and I step softly as we make our way up the crooked path to our right that mimics the dirt driveway leading to the cabin in question.

We crest the small hill and there it sits, a small cube of a cabin built entirely of logs with a wraparound porch and a river stone chimney crawling along the right side of the structure. It doesn't look big, two bedrooms at most. There's a peach glow emanating from the living room implying someone is home, but there's not a car in sight and no garage that I can see either.

Noah ticks his head for me to follow, and we boldly make our way right up to the base of the cabin. The two of us crouch low in an effort to conceal ourselves.

Beastly growls so loud I'm half-tempted to shush him, but thankfully, I remember the fact no one else can hear him. Noah and I aren't holding hands, so it's just me privy to his ferocious warning.

"See if you can go in," I whisper to him and Lea.

Noah turns my way. "Lottie, there are bars on the windows," he says it low, for my ears only.

"It's a prison," I practically mouth the words.

Noah motions for me to wait where I am as he slinks up the stairs—right next to Beasty and Lea, but unlike Noah, they hop right through the door as if it were open.

"They're in." I breathe a sigh of relief.

Noah crouches his way to the window and takes a brief glance inside before shaking his head my way.

I do my best to glide my way up the porch in the same covert manner and the steps squeak like mini alarms as I hit each one.

Perfect. I don't remember them squeaking when Noah went up, but then again, who could hear a darn thing over all the detonating my heart is doing?

"No signs of life," Noah whispers as I scoot in close.

"Mind your word choice. I'd swat you, but I might just shoot you by accident."

"Hold your fire. I have a feeling we'll need the ammo."

"Do you think she's asleep?"

"I don't know." He scans the vicinity briefly. "Where are your ghosts?"

I peer through the window and spot an ethereal glow coming from the hall.

"Deep in the house."

"Why aren't they coming out to give us an update?"

I shrug. "I guess I didn't ask them to."

Beasty jabs his head abruptly out the window next to us and I gasp.

"I heard that." Beasty offers a lethal sounding roar. "He's alone."

"He's alone!" I say it a touch too loud as I begin to dance to the front door and do my best to burst my way inside. "It's locked, Noah. Do something. Can you pick it?"

He runs his finger along the seam. "There's a bolt."

"Kick it down! Oh my goodness, he's here, Noah. We're going to save him. I just know it's not too late."

"Back up, Lottie," Noah pants as he holds me back with his hand.

In one svelte move Noah kicks in the door as if it were made of balsa wood. He pushes his way inside and I follow as the faint scent of flowery perfume infiltrates the air. The cabin is clean and sparse. A bowl full of apples sits on the small kitchen table big enough for two.

Noah and I make a beeline for the hall and I yank Noah into the room where Beasty's light is emanating from. I turn on the lights and feel faint when I see him.

Lying sprawled over a full-sized bed is Everett's enormous frame. He's shirtless, still wearing the pants he had on from his office that day. The scruff on his cheeks is bordering on a beard and his eyes are closed, his body perfectly still. His right hand and right leg are handcuffed to the metal bedframe.

Noah checks Everett's wrist. "He's warm. Pulse is good."

"Oh my stars." I hop onto the mattress and gently tap his face in an effort to rouse him. "Everett, wake up. I'm here. Noah and I are here for you. I love you so much. Please wake up for me." But Everett doesn't move. A low moan comes from him.

"Crap." Noah picks something up off the floor and holds it up my way. It's slender and white with a red tip. "She shot him with a tranquilizer dart."

"We're going to have to drag him out of here. How are we going to get the handcuffs off?"

"The fun way." Noah aims his gun at Everett's ankle.

"Noah, stop!" I look to Beasty and Lea. "Can the two of you use your superhuman strength to break these chains?"

Lea goes on the attack, gyrating her body wildly in the process, but to no avail. Her hair is back to covering her face once again and it really is an unnerving sight.

Beasty gives it a go as he tries to bite down over the bedpost, but nothing happens. "I may not be able to free him, but I can tell you with certainly there is a car approaching from down the road."

I look to Noah and nod. "Back to the fun way."

Noah ushers me into the hall and shoots nearly point-blank twice, and soon enough Everett is free from the bedpost with half the handcuffs still attached to his ankle and wrist. But my heart stops beating when I note the blood around his leg.

Noah hoists Everett up over his back with a grunt and we make a dash for the door. Beastly and Lea run ahead, and I lead the way to the truck where Noah dumps Everett into the back seat. Once we stuff him inside, we hightail it out of there. Just as we hit the cross street that leads to town, a small blue sedan drives past us with the shadow of a woman in the driver's seat.

"Noah, that has to be her."

"We don't have time to do an arrest. We need to get Everett to the hospital."

"Beasty," I say as I spot the oversized cat sitting directly over Everett's chest with Lea sitting over his back, her arms wrapped lovingly around him. "Take Lea and follow that car. See if you can memorize the license plate."

He leaps right onto the road, and I watch him jag like lightning until the evergreens block my path.

Noah dips his gaze to the rearview mirror. "Call the hospital, Lottie. Tell them we're bringing him in. He needs medical attention stat."

I'm quick to comply as Noah speeds us to Honey Hollow General Hospital where there is an entire team of doctors and nurses waiting to greet us.

Everett is going to be okay.

I hope.

CHAPTER 11

They say the happiest day of your life is your wedding day or the day you have your first child—but for me, knowing that Everett is out of the hands of that maniac—this, right here, is the happiest day of my life. Noah and I wait in the lobby while the doctors and nurses run a thorough examination. I called Everett's mother and sister with the good news, and despite the late hour, they're on their way to the hospital. I texted just about everyone I know to tell them the good news. I'm so elated, I'm about to float to the ceiling with sheer joy.

Noah flexes those dimples my way, no smile.

"What?" I recognize that sullen look. He's thinking about something, or more to the point, overthinking it. "What's wrong? Aren't you thrilled Everett is back? Please don't tell me that silly rivalry is rearing its ugly head again."

"Not that." He scoots in close. "Lottie, Everett is home and that's great, but the danger is still out there."

A mean shiver rides through me. "I'm secretly hoping once she sees he's gone, she'll pack up her things and hightail it to the Mexican Rivera for life."

"I wouldn't mind that either, but as evidenced, she's not well. She's obsessed. I've seen these things play out before. It's not always pretty."

"What are you saying?"

"I'm saying"—he bows his head a moment as if he were defeated—"we need to act twice as vigilant as we did before. This is either going to frighten her or embolden her to proceed with her plan."

"You can't be serious. There's no way she'd come after him again. He's not falling for whatever trick she used to get him in the car."

"I agree. And sometimes when you have a person who's unnaturally obsessed with someone else—and they realize they no longer have access to them—their only solution is to ensure that no one else has them."

An icy chill runs through my veins. "Noah." I shake my head, begging—*forbidding* him from going any farther with it. "We'll protect him. We'll hire the best security team out there."

"It won't change the fact that, until that woman is apprehended, he's vulnerable." Noah's features contort as if he were in pain. "And I'm afraid you are, too."

"You think she's going to come after me." I can hardly get the words out. "Of course, she is. She'll be watching us. Lurking in the shadows once again. She'll see how happy we are and she'll resent it. I'll be a target right along with Everett." Lainey pops through my mind. My sweet sister and her quickly approaching nuptials are in peril. "My sister's wedding. I can't go. I can't ruin Lainey's special day." Tears burn my eyes once again as I blink them back.

"Hey"—Noah wraps an arm around me—"I'm going to be there for you—for the both of you. There's no way in hell I'm going to let anyone hurt either of you."

I pull back, my lips quivering as I try my best to hold it together. "You really have the biggest heart of anyone I know. Thank you, Noah. I appreciate that."

A doctor emerges, and both Noah and I rise to meet him.

He's tall with curly dark hair and intense brown eyes. He does a double take Noah's way and inches back.

"You don't recognize me, do you?"

Noah's face opens with the slight look of surprise, and I can tell he's running a mental Rolodex as to who this might be.

"Morgan?" He inches back in disbelief. "Dawson? Morgan Dawson!" Noah laughs as he slaps the guy on the shoulder.

"Dr. Dawson to you, buddy." He socks him playfully on the arm. "I just heard from Alex. He says he's coming out here in a couple of weeks."

"We have to get together."

"Darn right, we will." He looks my way and offers an affable smile. "Dr. Dawson. Nice to meet you."

"Lottie Lemon," I say. "Nice to meet you, too. Can we see Everett? Is he okay? Has he come to?"

"Yes, yes, and yes. Whatever drug they gave him is quickly wearing off. He's in good health. His right ankle might be a little sore for the next few weeks. He's down that hall and to the right. It's good to see him. It's been a long time."

I bullet past him and Noah is right by my side as we storm Everett's room.

We find him seated upright, his eyes are glassy, but as soon as he spots us, his entire face lights up. There's a fortress of starry-eyed nurses tending to his every need, and I blow right past them as I lunge on top of him.

"Lemon," he whispers hot into my ear as I collapse my arms around him. "I love you." He presses a heated kiss to my temple, and I pull back with tears in my eyes. "How I've missed your beautiful face." He winces as he sits up a bit more.

The nurses stray out of the room, and Noah steps forward and slaps his hand to Everett's before going in for a hug himself.

"It's good to see you, man."

Everett's chest bounces, but there's a disbelieving look on his face.

"Come on. You loved it," Everett chides. "You had Lemon all to yourself."

Noah glances my way. "And all she did was talk about you, man. See? You cramp my style whether you're here or not." He leans in, his expression quickly sobering. "I'm glad to have you back. I mean that. What happened?"

His chest expands for a moment. "I was running late." His mournful eyes sweep to mine. "I was hoping to meet you at the lake. But court was running behind. As soon as I got my stuff together, I made my way out the building. I unlocked the car, opened the door, and just before I got in, I spotted something on my windshield. That's when she came around from the other side. She had a gun pointed right at me. Her hands were shaking. She asked me to toss my phone and briefcase into the bushes. I did as I was told, but I couldn't stop looking at her." Everett's deep blue eyes glide between Noah and me.

I nod. "Did she look like Harlow—Harlow James, the woman who was pregnant with your child?"

His lips curl slightly as he gives a slow blink my way. "I should have known you would already have this entire thing pieced together." He inches back. "How did you know that?"

Noah knocks his elbow in Everett's direction. "You go first. What happened when you recognized her?"

Everett winces. "I called out her name. She told me to get in the car and she would explain everything. And just like that, I found myself handcuffed to the interior of her car. She said her name is Hailey—Harlow's sister. She wanted retribution for ruining her sister's life." His forehead wrinkles as if reliving a bad memory, and I'm sure he is. "She also said that I should have been hers to begin with. That her sister stole everything from her, including me."

Noah and I exchange a look.

Noah is trying his best to process this. "We did a brief background check on Hailey yesterday. It's like she's a ghost. No carbon footprint whatsoever. It looks as if her father owns the cabin. The property taxes are up-to-date."

Everett shakes his head, baffled as he looks to the two of us. "So, how did you do it? How did you find me?"

"That was all Lottie—and you."

"That's right," I say, nestling beside him as I take a

seat next to his warm body, and, my goodness, how I've missed his warm body. "It sounds like you had Mangias and Wicked Wok delivered every day."

Everett's chest rumbles with a laugh. "Well, she was accommodating. It was all I could think of that might be a form of communication. But, I'll be honest, I didn't know if it would get me anywhere. However, I did know you'd be looking for me." He glances to Noah. "Both of you. Thank you." He wraps an arm around my shoulders. "She didn't hurt me in any way. She was making plans for the two of us to drive out of state. She wouldn't tell me where. She made it clear that we were together now and our old lives were dead." His features darken. "She asked about you." His finger caresses my cheek. "I spoke about you exactly twice, simply answering questions, and she grew aggressively irate, screaming, knocking things over. It was insanity on display. She had a bolt on the door that required a key, bars on all the windows, and the barrel of her gun trained on me whenever she let me out of that room. And when she had to leave, she chained me to the bed and shot me with a tranquilizer."

Noah sighs deeply. "It looks like you finally met your match."

"No," Everett is quick to answer. "This is my match." He warms my arm with his hand. "She was, and is, a psychotic mess. She's dangerous, Noah. And she needs to be stopped."

"She will be." Noah ticks his head to the side as if he were trying to speak to Everett in some secret language. "I'll make sure of it myself."

"I see," I say. "And you want me to stay out of this."

"Yes," they both say in unison.

Before I can protest, and they know I will, a couple of hysterically happy women sail through the door—his mother, Eliza, and sister, Meghan. They tackle hug him as I get bumped off the bed, and I watch with tears in my eyes as the happy reunion takes place.

Eliza is a socialite who lives in a ridiculously large department store she's trying to pass off as a mansion, nestled in the ritziest area of Fallbrook. Meghan lives in Fallbrook, too, and works insurance out there somewhere. They both share his dark hair and bright blue eyes.

"Essex, you've given us quite the scare." Eliza wipes the tears from her eyes.

Even though Everett's formal moniker is more or less reserved for those who have landed horizontally with him, his mother and sister are the exception to that rule.

"And I apologize." Everett takes them both in as if he never thought he'd see them again, and I'm betting he didn't. "I don't plan on letting it happen again."

"Good," Meghan huffs it out aggressively as if she were fighting mad. "Now where is the lunatic so I can say hello with my fist?"

ADDISON MOORE

"On the loose," Noah offers and they both moan in unison.

Eliza shudders. "Well, with you on the job, I just know she'll be apprehended quickly. Thank you, Noah, for bringing my boy back to me safely."

"It was Lottie." Noah nods my way.

My mouth opens as I look to him. "And it was Noah, too. He's just being humble. I couldn't have carried Everett on my back, down a hill, and to his truck. That was all you, Noah."

Everett inches back as he examines his former step-brother. "You did that?"

"Darn right, I did that. I wasn't about to leave you."

A swell of bodies burst into the room as a nurse does her best to hold them back. Mom and Mayor Nash, Lainey and Forest, Meg and Hook.

Mom rushes to his side. "Oh, thank goodness, you're safe! We were just at the Honey Pot having dinner when we got the news."

Mayor Nash steps up and shakes Everett's hand. "Glad to have you back, son. I'm going to do a press release in conjunction with the Ashford Sheriff's Department. I want the entire world to know what a top-notch job they've done." He looks to Noah. "Detective, expect a raise."

I can't help but bite down on a smile. Noah deserves the very best, and a raise is just the tip of the iceberg.

Lainey takes in a quivering breath. "Believe me, we're

all so glad you're back and safe. And I, for one, cannot wait to have you as a guest at our wedding. You too, Noah."

Meg belts out a laugh. "Hear that, Lot? It looks like you got your invite back."

"It must be true." I wink over at Lainey. "I heard it with my own two ears. Second best news I've got all night."

Forest purses his lips. "Any news on Jana March's killer?"

"What?" Everett growls it out low.

"That's right," Meg is quick to offer. "Someone shot her at the bridal convention. I bet it was a bridezilla gone ballistic." She smirks at Lainey. "It's been known to happen."

Hook gives Meg's shoulders a quick massage. "But don't anyone worry. I have full faith that the killer will be apprehended long before the wedding. In fact, let's not think about it. Meg says we've got a dance class tomorrow night."

"That's right." Lainey hugs herself as if she's trying not to think about the fact there's a killer on the loose, but it's not quite working. "The Underwood Ballroom at seven sharp. The class isn't exclusively for us, but Tracy is the best." My sister's chest bucks. "Jana highly recommended her."

Forest pulls her in. "Tracy is Pierce Underwood's sister. Pierce is—was—Jana's fiancé."

Hook nods. "Underwood Investments. That's right." He ticks his head to the side as if he still can't believe it.

"I'll be there," I say to Lainey. "Not only do I want to learn to two-step with the best of them for your big day, but I've been meaning to question Tracy."

Mayor Nash lets out something between a growl and a laugh. "That's our Lottie. She's quite the investigator, isn't she, detective?"

"Hear, hear." Noah grins my way.

Eliza picks up my left hand and runs her thumb over her mother's ring snug on my finger. "Well I, for one, encourage you to take all the ballroom dancing classes you want. With your own impending wedding at hand, you'll want to be sparkling in every facet on that glorious day."

"Yes," Meghan is quick to concur. "And when are we going to get a date out of you two?"

My lips part as I look to Everett for help. He's quite comfortable with his poor mother and sister believing the fact we're engaged. Everyone in here is in on it, with the exception of Mayor Nash. And come to think of it, my mother likes the idea of it so much—deep down, I think she believes it, too.

"We'll get back to you on that." Everett's eyes lock with mine as they offer up an apology all their own.

Noah chuckles. "Yes, well, I will be glad to help Lottie out tomorrow night. You just rest up, Everett, and get your strength back."

Eliza coos as she pinches Noah's cheek. "Aren't you just the best stepbrother anyone has ever had?"

"Yes, he is." Everett doesn't look amused. "Just the best."

The room breaks out into a dozen conversations at once, and just as quick as everyone showed up, one by one they say goodnight to Everett. It's just Noah and me left in the room with him, and neither of us looks as if we're in a hurry to leave.

"So now what?" I brush Everett's hair back with my fingers.

"Doctor says I'm cleared to go. Take me home, Lemon," he says as he winces his way to the edge of the bed.

Noah holds up a hand. "Not so fast. It's too dangerous for you to go back to your place. It's too easy. You'd be a sitting duck."

"Then he'll come to my place," I'm quick to volunteer. I like that idea much better anyhow.

Noah flinches as if I struck him, and I hate that he truly does feel that way.

"No way." Noah shoots the idea down without giving it a second thought. "There's no doubt in my mind she's already looking for you. Ivy texted a few minutes ago. The deputies are combing through the cabin as we speak. No sign of the woman who abducted you. She's already in hiding—or already back to stalking her prey.

Everett, you'll stay at my place until we get a better read on the situation."

"Noah"—I shake my head in disbelief—"that's incredibly kind of you. Of course, there will be no getting rid of me."

"Good." Noah's dimples dip in, but his expression is stern. "Because you're a target, too. Everett, you can take the guest room. Lottie and I will sleep in the master." A dirty grin spreads across his face.

"And here we go again," I say as I look to Noah and Everett. Just having Everett back makes everything else seem as small as a thimble. My heart feels full looking at the two handsome men in the room.

Noah, Everett, and I under one roof.

This should be interesting.

CHAPTER 12

*S*ummer in Vermont traditionally translates to wedding season. Sure, there are weddings in fall and winter, too, but they seem to be few and far between. And the rush on wedding cakes has never been busier than it has this July.

Lily shakes her head as we look at the six—count them *six* triple-tiered wedding cakes awaiting delivery this afternoon.

"I'm telling you, Lottie. That bridal expo has taken your business to the very next level. And don't think that it's stopping at weddings. I've already taken twelve orders for custom birthday cakes for this month alone."

"Oh my goodness," I pant as I try to catch a breath. "Thank goodness Keelie has lent me the staff from the Honey Pot to get these all out to the right venue. There's no way I can be everywhere at once. Who knew that pink champagne cake would be such a hit?"

"Well, there's no disputing it. I'm having a pink champagne cake at my wedding, too."

Wedding bells swirl through my mind and I think of Everett.

As much as I want nothing more than to cozy up with Everett and google the heck out of Hailey James, he sent me to work rather sternly this morning. I ended up baking a never-ending supply of pink champagne cupcakes today instead. I figure it will be easier for people to purchase them that way rather than by the slice. The little kids especially get a kick out of ordering them, even though all of the alcohol bakes out in the cooking process.

But the last hour was spent making sure these wedding cakes were sheer perfection. And I'm proud to say they are.

"Pink champagne." I shake my head. "You would think that's all we're capable of making. I can't believe there's not a request for a single other flavor."

"So, how's Everett? Rumor has it, the three of you are finally shacking up. Don't say I didn't warn you this would happen. It was just a matter of time."

Keelie squeals as she runs this way. "Don't you dare start." Her ear is already piqued in my direction. "Okay —shoot, Lottie."

I make a face at my best friend. "It's awkward. Noah insisted both Everett and I spend the night. We helped Everett get some things from his place, and I, of course, got into my nightgown and robe and picked up Pancake and Waffles. We put the litter box in his laundry room."

Keelie's mouth falls open. "What about his dog?"

"It took a few minutes of hissing and barking, but they all got along beautifully."

Lily lifts a brow. "And the boys?"

"There was some hissing and barking there, too, initially. Everett refused to sleep in Noah's guest bedroom. The bed was as stiff as a board and it was a twin. So Noah offered him the master bedroom and said he'd sleep on the couch. But Everett said, 'Sorry, sweetheart. I'm not touching your mattress. It might ruin my mojo.'"

Lily and Keelie belt out a quick laugh.

"So then, Everett slept on one sofa and I took up the other—with one eye open to just be sure it was real. I still can't believe he's back. And the courthouse was nice enough to give him the next two weeks off to recover."

Keelie bites down on a smile. "So, did you and

Everett sneak off into the restroom in the middle of the night and have some I'm-so-glad-to-see-you-again sex?"

"In Noah's house? Are you insane? I could never do that to him. It would break his heart." And mine.

Keelie gives a husky chuckle. "And that is exactly why Noah has you both under his supervision. He knew you weren't capable of indulging in hanky-panky with another man while under his roof."

"You're probably onto something."

Keelie swipes some icing out of the bowl with her finger. "What's up with Jana's killer? Do you really think we have two psychopaths running around Honey Hollow? Or do you think this woman who kidnapped Everett thought she was targeting *you* the day Jana died?"

Lily shivers. "As much as I like getting a paycheck, I have to admit, the bakery is starting to weird me out. I think we should hire a security taskforce to ensure our safety."

A man in a tan uniform catches my eye as he greets the customers entering the bakery.

"We won't have to," I say, nodding toward the deputy. "It looks as if Noah took care of that for me, too."

The phone in the office rings, and I step over and pick up the receiver.

"Cutie Pie Bakery and Cakery, Lottie speaking. Can I help you?"

"Yes, you can help me," a female voice whispers. "*Die.*"

RIGHT AFTER I closed up the shop, Noah swung by and we ran into Mangias for a quick bite before heading to Leeds for our ballroom dance lessons.

"I just feel terrible Everett is home, and I can't even enjoy him." My mouth falls open at the thought of those words actually escaping my lips. I'm sure Noah does not care to hear about how I'd like to enjoy his former stepbrother. "I mean, you know. His ankle is still pretty sore so he couldn't come out to the bakery today, and I was so swamped I didn't have a chance to check up on him in person. We've texted all day. He says you need a bigger TV, and he's pretty sure Toby will be going home with him when this is said and done—along with Pancake and Waffles."

Noah stifles a laugh as we pull into the parking lot of the Underwood Ballroom. I look out the windshield and gasp. There's a tall neon sign ready to greet us of a woman in a rather tightfitting ball gown. Her upper half consists of two round circles, twice as big as her head, and each one spins in a kaleidoscope of colors.

"What in the world? Why did I think this would be the classiest joint in Leeds?"

"Lottie, there is no classy joint in Leeds. You need to be trashy if you're going to survive in this town. This isn't your average dance studio. Yes, Tracy Underwood teaches classes, but she also has a ticketed viewing section. It turns out, there's a ballroom fetish and she's more than happy to fill their needs."

"Wow. You learn something new every day."

We head on into the oversized, over bright facility where a soft symphony of music is already playing. The peanut gallery consists of a couple of rows of folding chairs sparsely populated with men in trench coats.

A trench coat in July? I'm doing the fetish math, and I'm not loving it.

Lainey waves us over to where she's standing with Forest, Meg, and Hook.

"You came!" Lainey pulls me into a quick embrace. A tall woman with adorable comma-like dimples and dark hair that spikes out of her bun giving her a pineapple appeal walks by and Lainey yanks her over. "Tracy, this is my sister, Lottie. She just saved her boyfriend from a psychotic killer. You can bet your tap shoes she'll be bringing Jana's killer to justice soon, too. My sister is a crime-fighting superhero worthy of a cape. Isn't that right, Lottie?"

"Hardly." Note to self: Threaten everyone I know within an inch of their life to keep my sleuthing skills on the down-low.

"A pleasure to meet you." She extends a hand my way and I shake it. "Jana was a very special girl." Her left eye comes shy of winking and the facial quirk strikes me as odd. "She was everything to everyone. I can't imagine who would ever want to hurt her."

"Regardless," I say. "She didn't deserve what happened to her." She extends a hand to Noah. "And you must be the boyfriend. You are very lucky. Don't let this one go. A girl who would step in the face of danger for her man is *the one*."

"I agree." Noah gives a circular nod. "Lottie is definitely the one for me."

"And me," a deep voice says from behind and I glance back to find a devastatingly handsome man, clean-shaven, dressed in a freshly pressed suit with Cormack Featherby staunchly by his side. "That's exactly why I'm here." Everett holds out an arm and I thread mine through it. "Don't worry, Noah. I wouldn't dare let your dance moves go to waste. I've got a partner for you, too."

Cormack scuttles his way. "I don't know about you, but a good waltz always puts me in the mood to become the next Mrs. Noah Fox."

I choose to ignore her and steal a kiss from Everett instead. "You are a naughty, naughty boy. You're supposed to be resting."

His dark brows pinch. "And let Noah's hands have their way with your hips. Not on your life." A dark laugh rumbles in his chest. "I've missed you, Lemon. A herd of wild lunatics couldn't keep me away."

The music starts up and Tracy shouts at the crowd to

follow her lead, and thankfully I don't have to listen to Cormack's delusions for another second longer.

"Well, in that case, Judge Baxter, let's do this," I say as he takes up my hand and wraps his other arm around my waist. "You are a sight for my sore and tired eyes. And speaking of which, just about every woman in this place has her attention trained on you. So much for dance lessons."

His brows bounce, and there's a gleam in his eyes that inspires my stomach to bisect with heat.

"I've got my eye on the prize, Lemon, and that prize happens to be floating in my arms. What does a guy have to do around here to get you alone? There are parts of you I haven't had the pleasure to properly convey how much I've missed them." A scowl takes over his features. "Noah hasn't been trying to frost your cookies while I've been away, has he?"

A dangerous laugh brews in me. "Why, Judge Baxter, do I sense a smidge of jealousy in your voice?"

His chest bucks with a silent laugh. "Never. I don't let Noah Fox make me jealous, and I sure as heck don't let him tell me what to do. My place tonight, Lemon. My mouth has plans for your body, and I've got a few booboos you can kiss, too."

"*Ooh*," I squeal. "I don't know which amuses me more, the titillation factor or the part where you said *booboos*. But I don't think Noah will approve of us going to your place. It's still pretty dangerous."

His eyelids hood low, and his lips give a sexy curve as he comes in close and takes in the scent of my neck.

A dark moan emits from his throat, and just like that, his body is pulled back aggressively and Noah has an arm slung around half my body.

Noah pumps a dry smile. "If you don't mind, Everett, I'm cutting in."

Everett butts his shoulder into Noah's. "As a matter of fact, I do mind."

Noah growls as he tightens his grip on me. "Ah, yes, well. I carried your dead weight over a hundred yards to safety. I think you owe me one. And I'm ready to cash in." Noah adheres his torso to mine just as Tracy stomps her way over.

"No, no." She giggles. "Oh goodness, no. The waltz is a sophisticated number. We don't do threesomes."

Meg honks out a laugh as she and Hook swoop in close. "Lottie's a pro at threesomes!"

Hook nods. "We used to be, too. Those were the days." He winks as he gives my sister a dip. He had better be kidding. But I'm not too worried about it. Meg can more than take care of herself. And if I ever see Hook hobbling around in double leg casts, I won't ask any questions.

Tracy pulls a handkerchief from her bosom like a naughty magician. "One of you has to go."

"He's leaving," they manage to say in unison.

Cormack struts her way over. "What is going on over

he—" her left foot slips out from under her and she wobbles hard on her ankle as she struggles to right herself. "Ooh, ooh, *ooh*! Oh, Noah." She hops over—on her left foot ironically. "I'm afraid I'm going to have to ask you to take me back to the B&B." As fate would have it, both Cormack and Noah's wife are residing at my mother's bed and breakfast. "Oh please, I can hardly stand it. The pain is too much to bear."

Noah's grip on me loosens. "No problem." He takes a deep breath as he looks from me to Everett. "Don't stay out too late."

Everett offers him a mock salute. "Yes sir, Mr. Fox. I'll be sure to have her in by eleven." He leans in close to my ear and whispers, "In my bed."

Noah glowers at him as he helps Cormack hobble out.

The music picks up again, and soon the entire room is twirling and swirling to the rhythm as Tracy makes the rounds and adjusts arms, legs, and attitudes alike.

Everett and I glide by a hot pink curtain with the words *dressing room* clearly spelled out on a sign up above. And instead of sidestepping our way to the right, he steals me away behind that curtain before I realize what's happening.

It's small and cloistered in this glorified broom closet that doubles as an office. Lord knows I can so relate to that. There's a ginger jar lamp sitting on a messy desk strewn with papers and a box marked *uniforms* plopped on the floor.

Everett's brows waggle with devious intent as his hand glides underneath my dress.

A breath hitches in my throat. "You do realize once you get me going, I won't want to stop."

A dark laugh brews in his chest. "That's exactly what I'm counting on."

My mouth opens with surprise. "But Everett, there's just a flimsy piece of fabric separating us from the rest of the class."

"That's the best part, Cupcake."

I bite down over my lip as I pull him in close. "In that case, feel free to sentence me to whatever punishment—or might I say, pleasure, you see fit, Judge Baxter."

And Everett gets right to the task of doing exactly that.

Between the tugging of clothes, the hopping, the jostling, the downright nitty gritty of it all, a spasm of light catches my eye as a glorious tiger the size of my Honda appears standing on the desk.

"Beasty!" I say both excited to see him and embarrassed beyond belief.

"Beasty?" Everett quickens his moves. "I think I like that, Lemon."

"No, actually—" I slam into the wall a little too hard and the rod holding up that flimsy curtain falls to one side, and I watch in horror as the fabric glides slowly to the right as if teasing the peanut gallery for the big reveal.

Couples stop mid-flight, and the ballroom breaks out into wild gasps as I do my best to untangle my legs from around Everett's back and dismount to the floor. I pull my dress down in a fit as I spastically try to erect that curtain once again.

Tracy stomps over, partially fuming, partially amused. "Well, that's a new one." She clicks the rod back into place. "Please take a moment to put yourselves back together." She gives a sly wink my way. "Wrap it up, honey. I can't say I blame you. If that was my man, I'd be ducking into stray closets myself."

She closes the curtain behind her, and I can hear Meg shouting *way to go, Lot!* in the background.

"Kill me." I bury my face in my hands a moment as I scuttle to the left and bump into the desk.

"Nobody is killing you." Everett lands a kiss to my ear as I bite my lip from the sweet sensation. I glance down at the desk, half-tempted to rake it clean when I spot Jana's name written on a piece of paper.

"Everett, look at this," I say, pulling out my phone and taking a picture of it. "It looks like some kind of a receipt."

He pulls it forward, and we get a better look at it.

"It's not a receipt at all," he says, flipping it over, only to find the other side blank. "It's some kind of to-do list."

"That makes sense. They worked together." I take the

paper from him and point it to the light." Under Jana's name is an entire row of dates, and next to that nominal sums of money ranging from sixty to seven hundred dollars. "Do you think Jana owed Tracy money?"

"Anything is possible."

The music cuts out, and Everett and I head back into the ballroom, only to be met with a spontaneous applause led by my sisters. I'm so mortified I could drop dead. Speaking of which, that creepy phone call I got at the bakery earlier comes back to me. I haven't mentioned it to either Noah or Everett as of yet. I don't want to worry them. They're liable to team up and banish me from my own bakery. We already know that nutcase that kept Everett hostage knows where I work and live, and I'm not about to be another quasi-hostage of hers and live in fear by avoiding those two places.

The ballroom clears out. I say goodnight to both my sisters and their dance partners before Everett and I head over to Tracy.

Beasty flourishes to life once again and growls out a frightening hello.

"I just want to apologize for our behavior." I nod to Beasty because I was partially speaking to him. "We don't usually behave that way."

Tracy covers her lips with her fingers and gives a coy laugh. "I aspire to behave that way one day." She lifts a brow Everett's way. "You wouldn't happen to have a brother, would you?"

We share a warm laugh as Everett dashes her Baxter-based dreams.

"And again, I'm really sorry about Jana." I press my lips tight. "Jana was my friend, too."

She blows out a breath. "Jana was such a great girl. I don't know what my brother was thinking."

Beasty roars as if agreeing.

"Pardon?" I blink her way, trying to follow where's she's headed with this.

"Oh, you know, it wasn't any secret. He has a side girl he can't seem to get rid of. I told him, you've got a quality girl with Jana. You're engaged. That's not how you treat a woman." She shrugs and Beasty roars twice as hard as before. "But he let it go on for a little longer than it should have. I spoke to him last night, and we got into it again. He swears up and down he hasn't been with Monica for over a month." She wrinkles her nose. "But he's been engaged to Jana for two. Anyhow, I guess it's over any way you slice it. I sort of had this dream that Jana would be the one to finally straighten my brother out. I could see it now, the big house, white picket fence, two point five kids, the dog, the cat. Pierce is a good guy at heart. And now I'm afraid he won't meet anyone that nice again. Jana came from good breeding, you could tell. Monica—*pft*. She's a sleaze all the way." She takes a breath as she collects her bag from the floor. Her eyes connect with mine. "In fact, I wouldn't be surprised if it were Monica who did the deed. She never took too kindly to losing my brother to a glorified nun. That's what she called Jana." Her lips pull down. "I guess you could say Jana wasn't well-liked by everyone, after all."

Everett leans in. "Jana owed me money."

"You, too?" Tracy's jaw unhinges, and I give Everett's hand a quick congratulatory squeeze. "That girl didn't know when to quit. Sure, she was about to cash in with your sister's wedding, but the bulk of the payment was going to come in at the end. I was keeping her afloat for the last few months. She didn't want to ask my brother. Too prideful. She was afraid he would think she was only with him for his money. Please, every woman he's ever dated was with him for the money."

We walk out together, and she locks up the studio behind us.

Beasty jumps through the glass door as if it were a hoop on fire, and I bend over pretending to adjust my shoe.

"Any luck memorizing that license plate last night from the blue sedan?" That information alone could tell us more about the lunatic who thought she could get away with holding Everett hostage forever.

"It was covered with dirt." He gives a quick spurt of a growl as he tips his head toward Tracy. "Ask her about the loan repayment."

Everett glances around. I still haven't filled him in on Beasty, or Lea for that matter.

"Tracy, can I ask how you were going to have Jana pay you back?" I suck in my bottom lip a moment. And I'm asking this because? "Because she wanted to set up a strange payment system with Everett." That might work.

Tracy grunts. "Again? I'm telling you, the more I hear about her, the more I'm starting to think she was a scam artist. She wasn't exactly going to pay me back. And that fumed me, by the way. She didn't inform me of this, of course, until a few days before she died. She said she'd do my wedding for free." She holds up her left hand. "Do you see any rings on this finger? I'm not proud to say we had a disagreement just before she passed. I guess it's something I'll have to live with." She starts toward the parking lot, and we pause as we come upon Everett's car.

"Tracy? Where does Monica work?"

A dull smile slowly creeps up her cheeks. "The Disco Room. Two blocks to your left. Do yourself a favor and don't tell her you're investigating." She smirks. "The killer will outsmart you every single time with that information."

She takes off, and I wonder if the killer indeed just outsmarted me.

CHAPTER 13

"*I*s disco still a thing? It hasn't been a thing since the '70s, right?" I ask as Everett, Noah, and Cormack—of course, Cormack, my goodness, it's always Cormack—as we head into an all-black storefront with a plain black door. The only signage this place has is a spinning neon record that pierces ten feet into the sky.

"It's making a comeback," Noah assures me.

ADDISON MOORE

Everett leans this way. "Sort of like your relationship with Cormack."

I can't help but make a face. Everett got him there. It's seven-thirty, the weather is monstrously warm, and the air holds the scent of night jasmine. I'm guessing that fresh scent will soon be replaced with body odor once we enter through that grungy door.

The Disco Room, where Tracy Underwood pointed us to, is supposedly the establishment Pierce's inamorata, a woman by the name of Monica, works—read *dances*.

Both Everett and Noah are dressed to kill—and yes, that pun still slays.

Cormack has adorned herself in some number that consists of feathers peeking from her blouse. I'm not sure I have the time to analyze that properly nor do I care to. I'd ask how she came to be in our presence, but at this point I'm believing Everett. Noah wouldn't want her in his presence this much unless he wanted her. She's not really a stalker.

"I had a hard time keeping up." Cormack jabs Noah in the chest with her finger. "You nearly lost me at that last turnout, but I caught up as soon as we hit the Leeds county line."

On second thought, both Noah and Everett appear to have stalkers.

An egregiously loud roar thunders from behind as a tiger the size of a dining room table slinks our way.

"Oh good, Beasty's here." I finally filled Everett in on Beasty and Lea last night. He seemed both amused and mildly alarmed.

Cormack grunts. "Hear that, Big Boss? It looks like Lexi has her own special nickname for Essex." She frowns over at me a second. "Hey? Why don't you call him Essex? I mean, the two of you have done the deed, right?"

Everett sniffs as his chest expands with pride. "That's right, we have. Many, many savory times. In fact, we did it just last night at the dance studio."

My mouth falls open as I look to Noah. And suddenly, he looks as if he's not sure what exactly this deed consists of. It's best he be left in the dark. A tiny part of me still feels as if I'm cheating on him whenever I'm with Everett. And oddly enough, the opposite felt true when I was with Noah, too, even though Everett and I hadn't done a thing up until that point.

Beasty growls as he precedes us inside.

The rest of us head on in and are quickly accosted by the sound of the Bee Gees' "Stayin' Alive" on blast. The scent of burgers and curly fries permeates the air, and I'm hopeful I'll at least get a decent meal out of the deal. Just past the bright red reception area, it looks to be your average restaurant dotted with enormous round tables as far as the eye can see. The walls are lined with vinyl records, and there's a dance floor near the DJ booth up front, sparsely populated at the moment, but the night is young.

Beasty sits upright and his enormous head is just about eye level with mine. "Why do you humans insist on deafening yourselves with sounds that are clearly abusive?"

"Are you kidding?" My hips begin to shake as I snap my fingers. "This is amazing. It puts me in the very best mood." I wink over at Everett and Noah frowns. "It makes me feel as if anything is possible."

A waitress with a rainbow-colored wig that looks like an overgrown snow cone greets us with a smile. She's wearing a crop top that reads *disco inferno* and she's paired it with a gold lame skirt. There are so many fashion blunders taking place all at once, my poor eyes don't know where to look to catch a break.

"Welcome to the Disco Room! Do you have a preferred server?"

I suck in a quick breath. "Actually, yes. Is Monica in tonight?" Ha! And here I thought she was a topless dancer whom I'd have to bombard with questions after she shook her milk makers at Everett and Noah for the better part of an hour.

"Sure thing!" The talking snow cone is quick to usher us to a table near the back and Beasty sits in that invisible space between Everett and me. "Here are your menus." She hands each one of us a tall laminated ledger. "All we ask is that you keep menus, purses, and hands off the table until your server is through. She'll be out shortly."

I glance to Everett and Noah. "Strange instructions."

Cormack grunts. "As if I would ever put my purse on a table. I won't put it on the floor either. No sirree. You know what they say—purse on the floor, money out the door." She pats the seat between us. "Here, Logan, you put your purse next to mine."

I remove my tiny leather backpack with extreme caution as I set it next to me. It has my trusty gun in it, and heaven forbid Cormack should start digging around in there and accidentally on purpose misfire in my direction.

Everett's forehead wrinkles as he looks at the menu, inspiring me to glance at mine.

Meat torte, hot dog octopus, fondue, corn chip prune dip, tuna and waffles, pimento loaf cake, peanut butter potato salad, prune kebabs, gelatinous shrimp, baked bean mold, beef burger pancakes, ham and banana with hollandaise—the fun never ends.

"Hmm…" Cormack muses as she takes in the list of dicey offerings. "You know what they say. Ignorance is the parent of fear. I suggest we try a bit of everything."

Before the three of us could smack some sense into her, by way of her menu, the music switches up and Donna Summer's "Bad Girls" streams through the speakers at top volume.

A brunette with a heart-shaped face and her hair in

wild waves hops on over. She's wearing the requisite crop top paired with a gold lame skirt, and before I can scour her for a nametag, she steps over Cormack's thirty thousand dollar Birkin bag and hops onto the table.

"Oh my word." I scoot back in my seat as the enthusiastic table dancer twists and gyrates with the best of them. She does a high kick and the table tilts with her effort and both Everett and Noah grab ahold of it. The woman tosses her head left and right until her hair defies gravity, leaping in every direction like a dark flame. She drops to her knees, landing smack between Noah and Everett and whips off her top.

Holy mother of all things good.

I close my eyes a moment. Suddenly, we're seeing far too much of the breasty brunette. She shakes her maracas at Everett, getting a little too close to him for my liking, and I'm about to slide a menu between them when she bounces over to Noah and does the very same thing. The song wraps up and she somehow manages to touch her forehead to her belly button before tossing her hands—among other things into the air.

Cormack offers a spontaneous applause, and I'm slow to follow. At this point, I'd do anything to get the nude princess and her perky peaks off the table. In fact, I'm about to tip the table over myself when I note that Noah is leaning his head to the side with a newfound curiosity.

"Monica?" He tips his head back as his eyes grow wide. "Monica *Peeler*?"

Ha! Noah is so smart. He's clearly using a tried-and-true tactic where you spout off a fake last name in hopes they'll correct you and—

She stops cold as her mouth drops open. "Oh my gosh, *Foxy*? No-No? Is that really you?"

Everett slams his hand down over the table. "Monica Peeler."

She does a double take his way. "*Essex*?"

Cormack and I exchange a horrified look.

"Hey, hey, the gang's all here!" She's got an ear-to-ear grin that has no signs of letting up. Monica lets out a hoot as she brings both Everett and Noah into a rather chesty group hug. Since she's still hiked on her knees, she's a head above the rest and both Noah and Everett look as if they're being smothered with all that naked flesh. Not to miss out on the fun, Beasty wiggles his way into the mix.

Wow, he is such a boy.

In a moment of mercy, Monica hops off the table and pops back on her T-shirt, albeit inside out.

"So, what have you rascals been up to?" She gives Noah's ear a quick yank and it looked painful. I hope it was.

Everett points to Noah. "You called it, Monica. He's a glorified narc."

Noah averts his eyes. "And he takes pleasure out of locking people up."

She moans out a husky laugh. "Oh honey, some things never change."

Great. Not only does Monica recognize No-No and Essex, but I'm betting she's familiar with them both in the biblical sense.

Noah nods my way. "Monica, I'd love for you to meet Lottie Lemon and Cormack Featherby."

She gasps as she looks to Cormack. "*The* Cormack Featherby? As in Coconut Featherhead?" Something between a sneeze and scream emits from her mouth and... wait a minute. I think she's laughing. "Oh, I'm sorry!" She wipes her eyes with her pinkies. "But I'm brought right back to the days where these two used to war it out over you. So, who was the victor?" Her shoulders wiggle as she leans in to Cormack. "Let me guess. You're still taking them both for a ride."

"Future Mrs. Fox." She shoves her faux engagement ring at the girl. "And how, may I ask, do you know the boys?"

"My mother is the head housekeeper at the Baxter house. I grew up with Essex. That boy taught me everything I know." She gives him a cheeky wink. "The things we did in that laundry chute, in that kitchen pantry, in that dirty, *dirty* mudroom."

"We get the picture," I snip without meaning to. Oh heck, I meant it.

Everett winces. "Monica was the glue that kept Noah, Alex, and me together."

"And don't forget Meg Meg." She shoots Everett with her fingers. "She's my sister from another mister." She socks Noah on the arm, and again it looks like it hurt. "What's up? What brings you to a dive like this?"

Everett tips his head back as he looks to Noah. "Just taking our girls on a nice night out. What's edible around here?"

"The nachos. Let's face it. Nobody is coming in for the food."

Everett looks to Cormack and me and we shrug, indifferent to the questionable facts. It's safe to say we've lost our appetite about six minutes ago as we watched our dates get accosted by a topless blast from the past.

"Nachos it is." Everett nods her way. "What's going on with you? Other than strutting your hot stuff on tabletops? You seeing anyone? Married? Kids?"

She bleats out a laugh. "Darn right, I'm still hot stuff." She crashes her hip to his. "I'm dating a dog. No kids." She runs her finger down his tie in the shape of an elongated S. "You want to give me a little help in that department? We'd make a perfect pair. And your mother loves me."

"She loves me, too," I say, trying to sound cute and funny instead of desperate and insecure, but I'm pretty sure I hit those last two on the head.

"Aw." She gives one of my curls a tug—and yes, it

hurt. "You must be Sexy's little plaything." Nice to know he has a consistency with his nickname that spans decades. "Is this serious, or is it another case of two ships colliding magnificently in the night?"

"Lemon and I are a perfect combination of both. So who's this dog you're dating? Do Noah and I need to bust a few kneecaps?"

Noah and I? That bizarre brotherly camaraderie alone was worth the price of admission.

"An investor from Ashford. A real lunatic if you ask me. And that's exactly how I love my men. Right, No-No?" She gives his tie a yank, too, and soon she's got them both by the not-so-proverbial leash. "Ah, remember that night you and I got so drunk we sat on the roof and howled at the moon?"

"The good old days." Noah shakes his head wistfully as if he meant it. "So really, who's the dog? You never know. I might know him. Stranger things have happened."

She scoffs like she might be sick. "Pierce Underwood. A real piece of work. I'm not proud to say it, but I've been his side piece now for going on five years. He just glides in and out of other relationships, and I don't say a word. You know me. I don't think I deserve a man all to myself. My mother never did."

Both Noah and Everett start in on groans and moans and somewhat verbal protests.

She holds up a hand. "His chick died. Someone shot

her in the back a week or so ago. She's dead as a door-knob, and you know what that lunatic does?"

"He proposed to you?" Cormack's face is open with surprise as if it were the Cinderella ending every girl dreams about on the heels of a homicide.

"No." Her expression sours as Coconut Featherhead lives up to her moniker. "He starts sleeping with her best friend. I can't get my claws into this dude no matter how hard I try." She glances to the exit a moment. "And honey, I have tried more tricks in the book than I care to remember." The words come out weak as if she were speaking them to herself.

I force a dull laugh to tremble through me. "Like murder?" Okay, so it's not good manners to jest about committing a homicide when in fact an actual homicide took place, but we're all friends here, right? *Right*?

Her eyes narrow to slits as she hooks her gaze to mine. "There are a lot of people I'd kill for." She shrugs without adding another word to the ominous threat.

Noah sighs her way. "Did you know the girl? The one who was shot?"

She flicks her gaze to the ceiling. "Yeah, I knew her. Jana and I were actually friends. I mean, she didn't know I was sleeping with her fiancé, but outside of that we got along great. Heaven knows I liked her a heck of a lot more than I do his sister, Tracy, or the dead girl's best friend, Jackie. In my opinion, they should be slaughtered, too. Sorry to sound so crass. But Jana? Let's just say she got in somebody's way."

Beasty growls. "I don't like her. She's holding something back. I can see it in her lying eyes. Ask her if Jana borrowed money from her."

"Um"—I clear my throat—"did Jana ever borrow money from you?"

Her eyes spring wide open. "Jana didn't borrow money from me. She had Pierce taking care of her every need. It was me who needed money. It was me Pierce should have been throwing wads of bills at. Instead of living the high life, cruising on yachts, indulging on all the caviar and bubbly I want, I'm shaking my business at fifty different men a night. I'm sick and tired of being treated like the help and relegated to the back of the line. I went all in with my heart, and that man stomped on it time after time."

Beasty roars once again. "She's angry enough to kill. If she indeed harmed my sweet girl, I'll be sure to stomp on her heart until it stops beating just like Jana's."

"I'm pretty sure you're not supposed to threaten anybody," I try to say it low, for Beasty's ears only, but Monica sucks in a sharp breath.

"Honey, you'd threaten him, too, if you knew him. I'll be back with your order." She takes off and we take turns looking at one another after the rather odd breasty exchange.

Everett picks up my hand. "She didn't do it."

"You don't know that," I say. "You haven't seen her in years."

"True." Noah purses his lips. "But she didn't do it."

"Huh." I cast a stern look to the two leaders of the Monica Peeler Fan Club. "Would it be wrong of me to admit that this little bit of collusion between the two of you has moved her to the top of my suspect list?"

Noah's dimples flex at the thought. "All right, so she presented a clear motive, but she's not a killer." He winces. "But we'll explore the option."

Everett gives a sober nod. "It's the right thing to do."

Monica brings back a heaping platter of nachos and five plates as she joins us at the table, yucking it up with Everett and Noah as if they were back in high school all over again. Monica sheds a killer smile as she takes the two of them in. I can tell she's in yesteryear heaven. They all seem to be.

Cormack doesn't care for it.

I don't like it.

Beasty lets out a nonstop growl and a lesser-trained ear might think he was purring.

A lesser-trained sleuth—a transfixed old boyfriend— might think Monica was innocent.

But she had the motive to commit murder.

And I'm going to dig down deep enough to find out whether or not our chesty friend with a killer smile is a killer indeed.

We finally wrap it up, and both Everett and Noah dig

down deep into their pockets and leave a monstrous tip before we head out to the parking lot. Everett and I stop short as we get to his fancy ride, only to discover his windshield has been bashed in and reduced to rubble right over the driver's side.

We hitch a ride home with Noah and Cormack.

And all the way there I hold on tight to Everett.

She's still out there.

And she's not afraid to let us know it.

CHAPTER 14

The thought of spending the night with both Everett and Noah sounds more like a decadent fantasy gone awry than it ever would something seemingly mundane—but after we indulge in some delicious Wicked Wok and play a few games of Jenga, we each get ready for bed and exchange stories of our younger, far less wiser days. Noah and Everett share tales from the crypt, otherwise known as their high school years, in which Monica plays a starring role. I'll admit, it's refreshing to hear something other than Cormack's name for a change.

Toby snuggles up next to me on the couch while Noah holds Pancake, and Waffles lies over Everett's back. It's like summer camp, and I happen to have two of the cutest boys in my bunk.

I look to the two of them and bite down on a smile. "You know, if I didn't know better, I'd say the two of you were finally getting along. Who knew getting to second base with Monica on the very same night would be the tie that binds?"

Noah belts out a laugh and Everett moans.

"I wouldn't read too much into it, Lemon. The past is a nice place to visit, but it's not where we live."

Noah takes a deep breath. "He's right. We live here, under my roof because his bed-hopping habit caused him to pick up a psychotic. But lucky for me, that lands you here as well, Lot." He rocks back onto his elbows. "Do you realize we've been sleeping under one roof going on a couple weeks now?"

"And she's still not in your bed." Everett clicks his tongue. "I hate to break it to you, man. But you don't have her anymore."

Noah chooses to ignore him. "So, who's next on the suspect list, Lot?"

"Jackie. Both Tracy and Monica made her sound

dicey. If Monica is right and she's sleeping with Pierce, that makes me question her role in all this."

Everett tips his head my way. "I've seen grief drive people to do the unimaginable."

"Yes, Lottie"—Noah flashes a quick grin to Everett—"look whose arms you ended up in."

Everett huffs, "After she found out you had a wife? The blinders fell off. She's right where she belongs."

Noah bears into me with that forlorn gaze. "Are you?" he mouths the words, and I'm too mesmerized by his eyes to answer.

"I think we should stick to the case. We'll talk about Jackie tomorrow," I say as I drift off to sleep.

It feels strangely good like this with both Noah and Everett. It feels strangely safe—even if we're anything but.

"So, you haven't told Noah or Everett about that madwoman who called you up and told you to die?" Keelie blinks my way with an air of disbelief as we stand in the kitchen of the Cutie Pie Cakery and Bakery.

"Nope." I shake my head as I pull out another batch of pink champagne cupcakes. It's the morning after and I'm a little exhausted, seeing that Noah, Everett, and I stayed up well past my bedtime. I just finished relaying everything to Keelie as Lily walks into the kitchen.

"Lottie, your mother is here to see you."

We head out front, and I find Carlotta and an irate looking Greer Giles by her side.

"Lottie Lemon!" Greer bleats. "Who in tarnation gave you permission to put that little brat in charge of the B&B?"

I wince because it would seem my haunted sins have come home to roost.

"I can explain everything."

Carlotta inches me forward by way of her finger. "Can you explain why Harry Nash has invited me out on a dinner date?"

I gasp because I'm not sure which is worse: a child poltergeist haunting the B&B or my bio parents planning another hookup. Things didn't exactly go so well the first time.

Keelie waves as she heads next door. "I'm in on this next adventure, Lottie! Do not leave without me or I'll short your staff for the next solid week."

"I wouldn't dream of it." I pull Carlotta to the side, and Greer is quick to float along with us.

Greer growls as efficiently as Beasty. "It's bad enough there's a tiger with a terrible temper roaming those halls, but that kid you stuck us with? She's certifiably insane. She's writing 'leave or else" on all the mirrors in bright red lipstick. She's casting terrifying shadows and moaning far too loud in the night. People are downright frightened, Lottie! It's not cute, and it's not what the customers came for. Trust me, I know what they like. And once they start wetting the beds, you know things have gone too far. Your mother is going to have one stinky mattress mess in the very near future unless you oust that little twit."

"I can't get rid of her. She helped me free Everett. That was part of the deal. I told her if she got Everett back safely, I'd give her run of the B&B in exchange." My fingers fly to my lips with the impromptu confession.

Greer sucks in an unnecessary breath. "Lottie! Winslow and I thought you were our friend! Now where are we supposed to go?"

"Nowhere. Aren't the three of you gunning to be one big haunted family? You're the ones that wanted to adopt. Remember? You handpicked Lea, if I'm not mistaken. You finally have everything you wished for. You're welcome."

"AARGHH!" Greer roars so loud, the teacups rattle on their saucers as she disappears.

"That went well."

Carlotta makes a face. "So, what do you think? Should I go out with him?" Carlotta doesn't miss a beat, continuing our conversation from earlier.

"Mayor Nash?" I cringe at the thought. "You do realize he's my mother's boyfriend, right?"

"That's never stopped me before."

169

"Touché. But how about this? You ask my mother first."

"Miranda?"

"Yes, ask Miranda. And if she gives you her blessing, go for it. But, if she deflects in any way, back off. The last thing anyone needs is weirdness between the two of you. And, in my opinion, Mayor Harry Nash isn't worth getting weird about."

"Huh." She ticks her head to the side, and it's like looking in a mirror. Eerie. "Fine. I guess I'm off to talk to your mother."

"Sounds good. Hey, Carlotta?" I stop her as she heads for the door. "What made you change your mind about Harry? I mean, one minute you hate him and the next you want permission to go on a date. You can't have it both ways."

"Oh honey, I've had it both ways with that man for years."

I watch, sullen, as she takes off. I don't want that for my life. I don't want to be uncertain about love for so long. I want answers. I glance down at the ring on my finger. I want the wedding, the kids, the minivan. More than all of it, I just want certainty of what to do next.

Keelie bops back in and waves a key in my face. "I got a present for you."

"What's that? Don't tell me it's the key to my heart."

"Better. It's the key to the apartment Jana March

shared with Felicity. I talked Felicity into letting us look around. She says we can head over now if we want."

"We want." I hop to my feet and ask Lily to man the bakery as I hustle Keelie right out the back with me.

I may not be able to solve all the problems in the world, but snooping through Jana March's things will certainly make up for it.

CHAPTER 15

*J*ana March was roommates with Felicity Gilbert right up until she perished. I've already learned that Jana was having some issues with money and that both Tracy and Monica had motive to have her removed from the planet, but were they strong motives? Not in the least. I can't shake the feeling something else is going on here. Something bigger than money or red-hot jealousy over a shared lover—not that Jana knew she was sharing.

They say you can learn a lot about a person if you walk into their bedroom, such as their temperament, where their treasures lie, even the state of their mental well-being. I'm not sure what my bedroom would say, with its collection of patchwork quilts, the cozy over-stuffed comforter, the cat beds—which they eschew for my own—my shoes in a pile in the corner, and a stack of books that create a dangerous tower on my nightstand, but Jana's room—well, it looks pretty much straight-forward.

Keelie takes a breath. "I didn't know they made so many things with unicorns on them."

"It's a trend—a big one apparently."

Jana's walls are painted the faintest shade of pink with three large canvases of unicorns prancing in the woods, each one painted from a slightly different angle. Her curtains are bubblegum pink with unicorns and rainbows printed over them in a repeating pattern, and she has a matching comforter and pillow set over the mattress. There's a throw rug just below the side of her bed in the shape of a fuzzy white unicorn, and her desk is strewn with the mythical creatures in every shape and size.

Noah is working this afternoon. I didn't dare text him to let him know about the treasure trove I was about to walk into. And Everett's mother is taking him to lunch while his poor car is having its windshield replaced.

"Look at this." Keelie plucks a stuffed unicorn off the dresser with long iridescent strands for its mane and a silver lamé horn that spears from its head.

"At least she was consistent. It does look peaceful in here—if you're a thirteen-year-old girl."

"It makes sense, though. Jana was a hopeless romantic. She loved to make other people's romantic fantasies come true. She was living out her dreams with her event business. I admire her for that."

"You're right," I say. "I'll look around at the desk. See if you can find anything that might give us the leg up on the case."

"That's easy. I'll look in the trash." Keelie heads over. "I've been watching the Mystery Channel nonstop as a form of research. You're welcome, by the way. And they always find valuable clues in the trash."

"Good luck," I say as I quickly scan the books Jana has neatly lined up against the bookshelf. Lots of paperbacks, a smattering of hardbacks, all of them romances. It breaks my heart that Jana didn't live to get her own happily ever after. Pierce seems to have loved her—on the surface.

A picture of the two of them is set in a silver frame, and I can't help but snicker at him. "Here he is," I say, flashing the picture Keelie's way. I told her on the way over what a horrible person Pierce turned out to be.

"He's a cheat, a louse. I can't believe someone as sweet and smart as Jana got mixed up with a rat like this. He must have been a real con artist."

"Yes, well. It can happen to anybody." She shrugs my way, and that look on her face makes it clear she's referencing my own history with cheats. First Bear, then Curtis, then more questionably Noah—although, Noah didn't cheat on me, and I'm not entirely sure he was using me to cheat on his wife with. Noah and I were simply thrown into a complicated situation. The end. Only it's not the end. It feels more like the complicated middle.

A stack of journals sits in the corner, and I pull one over and gasp.

"Keelie! I think this is her diary. Look at the dates. It looks as if she wrote every single day. I do a quick flip to the back of the book, but the last date is over two weeks before she died. "Huh, she stopped a while ago."

Keelie bounces over and runs a finger over the seam of the journal.

"Oh my goodness," I say as we see it at the very same time. "Someone tore out the pages." I look to Keelie as our eyes lock. "Jana wrote something that incriminated someone, and whoever that was—they've already been here."

Keelie shakes her head, stunned in silence. "That's creepy, Lottie. But it has to narrow down the suspect pool."

ADDISON MOORE

"It does. I need you to get Felicity to casually tell you everybody who was in this room. I don't want to tip her off about the missing pages."

Keelie sucks in a breath. "Because you think she might have done it?"

"I don't know. I mean, I have to rule out everybody. One thing is for sure. I'm taking this with me." I don't hesitate putting the journal inside my bag. "Did you find anything in the trash?"

"Nope, just some receipts and a few to-do lists. Jana was an infamous list maker."

"Don't I know it. I'm still trying to chew through that folder Lainey gave me. In between writing all those lists, I don't know how Jana got anything done."

Keelie hands them over, a stack of notes on a small yellow sheet of paper, each one labeled with the date at the top. Most of these items are things you wouldn't even think to put on a list like, *grab coffee at the bakery*, but I'm humbled and honored to have made her list in some small way. Her fiancé is predictably on just about every list—*dinner with Pierce, lunch, breakfast, movies, the lake…*

"Hey…" I shake my head as I note a loss to the pattern. "Pierce is a staple on all of these, but exactly two weeks before she died, she stopped including him in her daily byline. The last time he was mentioned was on a Tuesday. It says *noon, surprise Pierce with a picnic lunch.* And then nothing after that."

"Ooh." Keelie leans in. "Maybe she caught him with another woman."

"I don't know. She was holding his hand at the convention and she introduced him as her fiancé."

"Well, maybe they made up? Couples go through rough patches. Maybe this was theirs." She points to the rest of the list. "Besides, it looks like her business was picking up steam. She was really gearing up for that bridal expo."

"You're right. I think maybe we should go." I take all the to-do lists I can find from the trash and shove those into my bag as well. "You were right, Keelie. The trash can prove to be a treasure trove of goodies."

"You know what else is a treasure trove of goodies? The sock drawer and under the bed."

"You take the bed and I'll take the sock drawer." I head over to her dresser, and sure enough the top drawer splits in two between her unmentionables and socks. I quickly rummage through the sock portion and come up with nothing but a pair of mismatched socks with unicorns printed on them. I do a quick swish through her unmentionables, and my hand hits something hard. I pull up a tiny jewelry box.

"I think I found something." I open it up and gasp. "Keelie, this looks like an engagement ring." We stare down at the enormous emerald cut diamond as it glistens and winks our way.

"Don't you think it's odd that she didn't wear it to the bridal expo that day?"

"Huh. Maybe this is something else? Another gift her boyfriend gave her? He's apparently loaded." I put it back where I found it, and we take off.

I drop Keelie off at the Honey Pot and head on down to Ashford.

I have Jana March's journal, albeit the juicy bits removed, her to-do lists, which have more line items for a twenty-four-hour period than an average person expects to get done in a month, and an itch to discover if her ring finger was bare.

I have a feeling there's a certain detective that might just help me scratch that itch.

Jana March's killer should be getting very nervous.

I'm closing in on you, whoever you are.

You can run, but you can't hide.

I'm coming after you.

CHAPTER 16

he Ashford Sheriff's Department is a white boxy building that welcomes me with its blissfully air-conditioned arms. It's so boiling hot out, I'm sure I lost ten pounds walking from my car to the building in perspiration alone. Inside, it holds the scent of burnt coffee, the floors are white linoleum, and the walls echo the same snowy hue. I follow the hall to my right and give a quick knock on Noah's office door.

He looks up over his glasses before plucking them off. "Lottie Lemon." His dimples dig in deep at the sight of me and his eyes soften as he takes me in. "Please tell me you come bearing sweet treats. My stomach is rumbling something fierce."

I wince. "Sorry. I sort of came over in a hurry."

He points to the seat in front of his desk and I take it. Noah's suit jacket hangs from a hook on the wall, and I can see his gun holster strapped around his shoulder as it circles to his back.

Looking large and in charge, Noah is handsome and sexy as anything behind his big black desk. Sometimes I wonder what life would have been like if Britney wasn't in the picture. Would Noah and I have been married by now? I'd like to think so. And if we were, I'm sure this would quickly morph into a conjugal visit.

"Where's Everett?" He glances to the door as if fully expecting to see him.

"Having lunch with Eliza. He's having his windshield fixed later today, too."

Noah tips his head to the side. "Any lions or tigers or bears with you this afternoon?" He does a quick visual sweep of the room before his eyes meet up with mine again, this time inspiring a sweet smile.

"It's just me. I'm sorry if that's a disappointment to you," I tease.

"Are you kidding? You just managed to turn my day around with a smile. So what's up? Are you hungry?"

"I'm starved."

"Good. We'll go to lunch."

"That sounds perfect, but first would you mind if I went over a few things with you?"

"Shoot."

And shoot I do. I tell Noah about Keelie's surprise—the search of Jana March's bedroom, the diary with its missing pages, the to-do lists, and the emerald cut diamond the size of a quarter.

"Lottie"—he sighs as he thumbs through the to-do lists I've handed over—"legally I shouldn't have all this evidence in my hands without the proper search warrant, but since you were not technically breaking and entering, I'm going to overlook the fact you took things from her bedroom without garnering permission first."

"From whom? The deceased? I'm not asking Pierce, that's for sure. That apartment is technically Felicity's and all the things in it, too, including this." I plop Jana's journal in front of him, and he inspects the ripped seam where the pages were ripped out, jagged. "Keelie is going to find out from Felicity who else had access to Jana's room since she died. Noah, I need to know if Jana had an engagement ring on when she was killed."

"Easy." He picks up his phone. "I'll call the morgue."

It takes less than ten minutes for Noah to get a complete report sent to him on the items Jana had on her person the afternoon she was killed.

ADDISON MOORE

"Two bracelets, one pearl necklace, a matching set of button pearl earrings, a toe ring, sandals, a dress, bra, underwear, an elastic band in her hair." He glances up. "No ring."

"No ring." I nod. "Why in the world would Jana not wear her engagement ring? I mean, I'm not engaged, but I've hardly taken off this ring Everett's mother gave to me. I'm terrified I'll lose it. Which reminds me, I really need to give this back to Eliza, but I can't seem to figure out how. But you know what? When I do take it off, my finger feels naked without it. Of course, when I bake, I take it off and put it in the ground safe at the bakery. But Jana was at a bridal expo. You'd think that would be the perfect place to wear it."

"It is." Noah tips his head to the side. "Whatever happened in her journal that last week would have either pointed us to the killer or to a motive. Jana obviously was busy that last week, so we may not be able to read too much into the fact Pierce took a back seat, but that ring... I just wish we knew what the last few pages of that journal said."

"I glossed over the entire month before, and she was gushing over her engagement and her new job as my sister's wedding planner. She even talked about how much she loved Honey Hollow." A thought comes to mind. "Wait a minute. Jana and those last few pages of her journal might be gone, but I have a feeling there's a talking journal out there that might be in the know."

"Such as?"

"Her best friend. I think we should head over to Underwood Investments and have a chat with Jackie. Which is perfect timing because she's the next person on my list."

Noah's forehead creases with worry. "I'm wondering if she'd open up to me again. I'm the one that questioned her the day of the killing."

"What did she say?"

"Nothing suspicious. She seemed devastated."

"Huh. We ran into her at Mangias a few days later and she looked just fine. She was probably holding it together, trying to help Pierce manage his own grief. Funny thing about grief, though—it's an appetite killer. They were both enjoying a feast just days after the killing." I shake my head. "That was a lot of conjecture and harsh judgment, wasn't it?"

"It was, but that, my friend, is the long thorny road to catching a killer." He jumps up and puts on his jacket. "Let's drive down to Underwood Investments. It's about a block away."

"Perfect. How about we stop off at that donut shop down the street first?"

"You really are a homicide detective in the making, you know that?" He chuckles at the thought.

"Not for me, for Jackie. If I've learned anything, the way to the truth often starts with something sweet to eat."

WE PICK up the donuts—two boxes, one for Noah and me and one for Jackie and the rest of the employees at Underwood Investments. Noah and I eat three each before we drive by and indeed spot Jackie at her desk through the window.

We park a few paces back from the office, and I head on in with an apprehensive smile.

"Knock, knock," I say as I wave over at her.

Jackie's entire face brightens at the sight of me. Her hair sits over her head like a dark nest, and she's wearing oversized purple-framed glasses that offer her an adorable appeal.

"I'm sorry." She winces. "Is it Lizzie? I'm terrible with names."

"Lottie." A warm laugh bubbles from me. "It's not your usual name, so I don't hold it against you. Besides, you're still grieving." I set the oversized pink box of donut deliciousness on her desk. "This is for all of you. I'm sure it's been tough around here in general," I say, taking a seat in front of her.

"You don't know the half of it." She pulls the box over and dives right in. "Mmm," she moans, taking a bite out of a fresh glazed donut. "It's still warm. You're the best, Lottie. Thank you."

"No problem. Any news on the arrangements?"

"Funeral is Wednesday at that church up in Honey Hollow."

"Oh, I'll be sure to send some baked goods over to go along with the refreshments in the aftercare area. Free of charge, of course. Have you thought anymore on who could have done something like this?"

She shakes her head. "I can't get it out of my mind, and yet I'm baffled. Do you realize that sweet girl didn't have an enemy in the world?"

"I believe it. So, someone must have wanted something from her. Money maybe?"

"She didn't have two dimes to rub together." She takes another bite.

"But her boyfriend was rich, right?" I glance around. "I mean, maybe it was someone trying to get to him?"

She inches back as if it were absurd. "I don't think so. It's pretty mellow around here. Or it used to be before Jana died. It's been utter chaos ever since with Pierce practically ghosting this place. His head just isn't in the game anymore."

"What was she like—that last week before she died? Did anything seem off to you?"

Jackie tips her head to the side thoughtfully. "You know, she was a little quiet, withdrawn, but that's exactly how she would get when she threw herself into her work. Your sister's wedding was her biggest event to date. She was really hoping it would help launch her

185

wedding planning career. The poor girl needed a break, and she certainly didn't get one."

"No, she didn't."

A spasm of light erupts behind her, and a giant white tiger jumps right onto her desk before landing to the floor with a thump.

Jackie's face smooths out. "Was that just an earthquake?"

"Huh? I didn't feel anything." I shoot Beasty a look.

"Get rid of her," he roars it out low. "She's hiding something. I can feel it."

I shake my head his way.

I can't get rid of her. This is her office.

Geez. He really is ornery.

"Is something wrong?" Jackie leans forward.

"Oh no. I just thought... the rest of the people in the office might want a donut while they're still warm." So lame. As if she's really going to fall for that one.

"Steven's in the back. I'd best deliver these, lest I eat the whole box. Just a second." She takes off with the pink box, and my mouth falls open.

"Look on her desk," he grouses. "Something is there."

I lean over and do a spastic scan of the vicinity, a couple of legal pads with notes confirming clients, a magazine opened to a page with a picture of a swimming pool, a couple of coupons for the coffee shop down the street, a calendar. I crouch over her desk to get a better look at it and note every brick of time is filled straight through this week and next—and then I see it. A big fat circle with an X through it around the day after the funeral. The words BIA.

Burlington International Airport. That's right. Pierce is off to Greece to sail around the Mediterranean with his friends.

Jackie comes back, and I fall hard into my seat.

"You're officially Steven's favorite person," she beams.

"They do say the way to a man's heart is through a warm donut."

She laughs as she falls back into her seat. "I'll have to remember that."

"So, how is Pierce? I bet he's looking forward to getting out of town."

She shakes her head. "He's changed his mind. Actually, I managed to change it for him. He's not leaving for another few weeks. We still need him around here. I still need him." She says that last part almost to herself.

"Do you think the rumors were true?" I manufacture a pained smile. "You know, that he was cheating on poor Jana?"

Her eyes enlarge. "Who told you that?"

"You know how Honey Hollow is. It's such a small town, everyone knows everything. It's just a shame that Pierce didn't think Jana was enough."

She swallows hard as she reaches for a water bottle. "It's funny, in the beginning I was madly attracted to

187

him. Then Jana started working with his sister on one of those wedding planning gigs when Pierce and I walked in. I saw her eyes light up, his eyes lit up, too, and the rest is history."

Huh. That's not quite the story I remember her telling—at least not in that order.

"But you couldn't date him anyhow. That whole no dating employees thing, right?"

Her chest bumps with a laugh. "It's what I tell people to save face. Steven's girlfriend helps with the accounting."

She means Kelleth, my new half-sister, and my nose wrinkles at the thought of her.

"That's surprising for such a huge organization. I mean, entrusting one person with such a big job. You must have hundreds of employees."

She shakes her head. "Nope. It's just the four of us. A pretty small time deal. We're still killing it, though."

My antennae go up. Something doesn't sound right. Hook seemed blown away at how big this place was.

"Well good. As a business owner, it pleases me to hear that other small businesses are thriving, too."

I rise to leave. "I'll see you at the funeral."

"And at your sister's wedding," she says through a mouthful. "Jana asked me to help with a few details—you know, before she died"—she whispers that last part—"and, of course, I agreed to it. I'd do anything for that girl."

"Oh, I'm surprised there's anything left to do. I've got a list a mile long myself."

She waves it off. "I've got some Grecian columns she had stored in my garage and she asked me to help schlep them over. Pierce was supposed to help, and I'm going to make him as one last act of kindness to that girl."

"That's sweet of you both, but if it's too much just give me a call at the bakery and I'll have it taken care of."

I take off for Noah's car and close the door to keep the pressing heat out.

"What happened, Lottie? What did you learn?"

"I'm not sure, but I think Jackie has the hots for Pierce. And I'm not entirely sure Hook knows anything about Underwood Investments."

"Redwood Realty is just down the street. We can ask him ourselves."

"Let's do it. After we enjoy another quick donut break."

"Ah, a detective after my own heart." He gives a light-ning quick wink. "You already have it, Lot."

"I know," I whisper and we tap our donuts together as if we were toasting.

Noah has mine, too, right along with Everett, and I'm entirely baffled as to how I let this happen.

CHAPTER 17

Redwood Realty is on the corner of a shopping plaza nestled between a pizza parlor and an automotive repair shop.

Inside, it's reasonably cool. The floors are a glossy black granite, and the furniture is gray with white marbled countertops. Noah and I ask to speak with Hook, but the secretary lets us know he's with a client at the moment.

A familiar high-pitched voice of a woman tugs at my ear as I give Noah the side-eye.

"That sounds just like Lainey. I'd bet my life that was my sister," I say as I take a step beyond the wall to my left, and sure enough I spot Lainey and Forest seated across from Amanda Wellington. She's not only one of Redwood's premier realtors, but she was a competitor of Jana's—the exact competitor Jana was arguing with the day she was gunned down. "Well, what a surprise," I say, pulling Noah in with me.

A spray of white light flashes from the ceiling and down drops Beasty over the desk with a roar.

Now *that* was a true surprise.

"Not without me, Lottie," he grumbles as he hops to the floor.

"*Lottie!*" Lainey jumps up and gives me a firm embrace. "Hey, Noah." She gives a quick wave as we say hello to everyone in the office.

Forest is dressed in khakis and a crisp baby blue shirt, not his usual day off from the firehouse attire. And Amanda looks stunning in a floral silk blouse, her red hair framing her face softly.

Lainey glances back to Forest. "Should we tell her?"

"Your call."

Lainey spins my way. "We just made an offer on a house!" she squeals as she hurdles herself on top of me once again.

"Lainey! That's great. Congratulations."

Amanda clears her throat, a smile already on her lips. "They don't have it just yet, but the offer is strong and the seller is anxious to move on. I think it's safe to buy the champagne."

"A wedding *and* a house." Noah slaps Forest a quick high five. "Congratulations, man. You're living the dream."

"That I am. Just one more week and I'll be a married man. I cannot wait."

"And"—Lainey tips her head my way—"thanks to your new brother, we have a spectacular deal on a cabin up at the Sugar Bowl Resort. I'm so excited—I'm already packing." Her fists ball up with glee. "Oh, and don't forget, both you and Meg have to run over to Scarlet Sage by Thursday and try on your bridesmaid dresses. That still gives her plenty of time if she needs to do any alterations."

"And what about you? When is your final fitting?"

"Thursday at noon, but she's actually doing the fitting at Mom's. That's where the dress is. Hey? I'll have her bring your dresses, too. We'll have lunch after." She lifts her shoulder as if the thought made her cheeky.

"You couldn't keep me away."

Both Lainey and Forest say a quick goodbye to Amanda as they make their way out of the tiny office. Noah pulls them both to the side and starts in on a conversation about the wedding.

Perfect. Noah is so intuitive to what my needs are,

it's as if there were two of me running around the planet.

Beasty lets out a low, yet intimidating growl as if to say *hop to it*.

"So, Amanda?" I crane my neck back into the cubicle as I take a step inside. "How's everything going? The bakery has exploded with business after the expo."

"Same here." She picks up a white lace fan off her desk and begins cooling herself with it. "And sadly, I've picked up every last one of Jana's clients. But I'm more than glad to do it."

"Things looked a bit tense between you and Jana that day." I press my lips tight. "Do you think she was stressed about something? Like maybe she knew she was in trouble?"

Amanda rolls her eyes. "I don't think so. And I'm embarrassed to say what we were arguing over. It all seems so petty right now." She waves it off.

"No, go ahead. I mean, you never know—talking about it might actually jog your memory and unlock something that might help Jana's case."

"I doubt it." She slaps her fan closed and leans in. "All right, this is what our little tiff was about. Jana interned for me last summer. I had noticed pretty early on that I was losing clients to her, but it wasn't until the expo I learned the truth. It turns out, they were still contacting Jana for events and she forgot to leave off the little detail that she no longer worked for my company. That little weasel was siphoning off my clientele. I hate to sound crass, but that was a low-down and dirty thing to do. And even though I'm sorry she ended up dead, she certainly had something coming to her."

"So you thought she stole your clients?"

"Oh, she did. She admitted it, too. She said once she was on her feet she was going to float a few back to me, but everyone knows the big events, the weddings, the anniversaries, the big birthdays only come around once in a blue moon. I was livid with her. She's the kindest soul on the planet, so to see this ugly side of her rear its head really threw me for a loop. But like I said, I've got them all back now. All's well that ends well." She gives a sly wink.

Only it's not ending well for Jana.

Jana is dead.

Beasty lets out a deafening roar as if he were thinking the very same thing.

Lainey pops her head back in. "Aren't you here to see Everett?"

"Who?" I say a quick goodbye to Amanda as I dance back into the hall. "Did you say Everett? I was here to see Hook."

"You're in luck." Forest takes up Lainey's hand. "They're actually in there together." He points toward a bona fide office with Hook's name written across the front.

"I'll catch up with you later. We're off to celebrate,"

Lainey chirps as they head on out, and I make my way to where a trio of familiar voices stem from. Sure enough, Hook sits at one end of the oversized desk while Noah and Everett are crouched looking at a laptop screen on the other side.

"It looks like I'm late to the party."

Everett rises and greets me with a kiss. "There's not a party I want to be at that starts without you, Lemon."

A dark laugh bounces through me. Everett always knows the right thing to say. "What are you doing here?"

"My car is next door. I just finished up lunch with my mother and had her drop me off. And to kill some time, I wandered in here and asked Hook if he'd help me figure out if whoever owned that cabin held more real estate in the area."

"That's brilliant." My cheeks flush with heat as Everett presses his blue-eyed gaze into mine.

Noah glances back. "It's her father, I'm guessing. And yes, there are three additional properties, but they're all currently rented out to other people. Everything checks out so far. And I still haven't been able to get in touch with him regarding Hailey. I've left several messages for him to call me back."

I twist my lips up at Everett. "Any other incidences?"

His eyes flit to Noah and they exchange a quick look. "What?"

"She sent a bouquet of black roses." He shrugs. "To Noah's house."

"Great." I close my eyes. "I suppose this would be a good time to mention the threatening phone call I received a few days ago."

"A few days ago?" Noah growls it out. "Lottie, are you insane? You cannot wait to tell us these things."

"He's right." Everett's brows dip down like birds in flight. "I'm sorry you have to go through this."

"Don't apologize to me."

"What did they say?" Noah's tone is demanding and for good reason.

"They told me to die." I clear my throat as I glance to Hook. "Not to change the subject, but can I ask you a question about Underwood Investments?"

"Anything." Hook reclines into his enormous leather seat. "I'm familiar with them."

"You mentioned you thought they were a big operation, right?"

"They're huge."

"I thought so. But I was just there and the secretary said it was just the four of them."

Hook's cheek twitches as he considers this. Hook is handsome to a fault and a nice guy to boot. I couldn't be happier for Meg.

"It's probably a satellite office."

"I see, that's probably what she meant."

We wrap it up and head next door, only to find out Everett's car still has an hour to go so we head to the pizza place a few yards over.

"Suspects," Noah says as he picks up a slice of steamy hot pepperoni pizza. "Let's go over this, Lot. I bet the three of us could tease out a killer if we try."

I make a face out the window. "I don't know. This is a tough one. We've got Pierce—who is a lowlife snake that I've lost all respect for. I would never put my money in his investment company. I bet he cheats on his money, too."

"Hear that, Noah?" Everett flexes a short-lived smile. "She doesn't like a cheat."

I tick my head to the side. "Tracy—Jana owed her money, and Tracy seemed pretty upset about it, too. But she seemed angrier about her brother's behavior. Jackie —Jana's best friend. It's clear she's still interested in Pierce. But maybe she figures now that Jana is gone she might have a chance?"

"Because she killed her?" Everett takes a bite out of his pizza.

A thought comes to me. "Hey, Jackie seemed to know about Pierce's cheating when I talked to her about it this afternoon. What kind of a best friend would keep something like that from her?" My mouth falls open. "The kind that wanted to get in on a piece of the action. I don't think Jackie was Jana's best friend, after all."

Noah nods. "More like her worst friend."

"Her worst friend," I echo. "Which brings me to another lousy buddy—Amanda Wellington. She told me that she accused Jana of stealing clients the afternoon she died, and that Jana admitted it. No wonder they were arguing that day. Amanda would have had plenty of time to kill her and get back into the venue. She was certainly pumped up with enough anger. But honestly, I just don't see any one of these people angry enough to kill Jana—and in broad daylight at the bridal convention of all places."

Everett casts his gaze to the wall. "What better place? Think about it. All of the suspects had a motive. The killer might have wanted it that way. It certainly takes the spotlight off one person."

"They didn't even have to lure her there." The words come from me breathless. "Unless it was a crime of passion, Jana was a sitting duck."

Lainey's wedding is less than two weeks away, and I'd do anything to have this killer behind bars before then.

Who killed you, Jana?

Who?

CHAPTER 18

ana's funeral was officiated quickly and simply by Pastor Gaines, the new hire at Honey Hollow Covenant Church that my mother seems to have taken a liking to as evidenced by the fact she's dangling all over him now that we've moved to the reception area next door in Carlson Hall.

There's a large framed black and white picture of Jana's smiling face that was moved over from the sanctuary a few minutes ago, and Beasty sits staunchly by her side, his chin up as if he were guarding her with pride. Each time one of the suspects gets near him, he belts out a horrific roar. His love for her is so sweet it makes my heart ache just witnessing it.

Both Noah and Ivy are walking around separately, trying to look casual while listening in on various conversations. It sounds deplorable, trying to get dirt that way, but I think we're all anxious to put this mystery to rest.

Everett nods toward the door. "That looks heated."

I turn to find Pierce and Steven having what looks to be an extremely intense conversation.

"I bet Steven's not thrilled with the fact Pierce still wants to take an extended vacation. I can't say I blame him for wanting to get away."

"But I can see Steven's point of view. They've got a business to run."

"I don't know. Hook says it's a huge outfit."

"But you don't think so?"

"Jackie said it was just the three of them—four if you count Kelleth. Although, Hook did think it was just a satellite office."

"Maybe we should dig into that?"

I'm about to agree when Mom hightails it my way, looking as if she were about to pass out.

"You didn't book the church."

"Book the church for what?"

"Lainey's wedding!"

"Why would I book the church for the wedding? I mean, wasn't that done months ago?" I scan the vicinity and find Lainey chatting away with Keelie and Naomi.

"Yes, it was done months ago, but it was supposed to be confirmed and the deadline passed. The secretary just told me that when she couldn't get in touch with the wedding planner she figured they changed their minds. She booked a funeral for the same hour as Lainey's wedding!"

"Oh my word, this is horrible. This is all my fault. It's probably on that mile-long list I've yet to tackle. Can't they just move the funeral? I mean, it's not like the deceased has anywhere to go."

She closes her eyes, clearly indignant with my response.

"No, Lottie, they can't."

A viral panic begins to set in. "Okay, okay! Please don't tell Lainey any of this. I'll figure it all out."

I turn to find Everett gone from my side, and a whole new panic begins to sink in.

"Everett?" I take off without saying another word to my mother. My heart vibrates right up into my throat, and just as it's about to eject itself, I spot Noah, Ivy, and Everett in the parking lot. I head their way and stop short before I get there.

Everett's rear window was taken out this time—with bits of broken glass spider-webbing just like before.

She's struck again.

She's getting bolder—far more dangerous by the hour.

Someone has to stop her.

But how?

THE AFTERNOON of my sister's final fitting for her wedding dress has Meg and me both slinking into blush pink floor-length chiffon dresses with sweetheart necklines and capped sleeves. The conservatory at my mother's B&B is empty, save for the four of us.

"It's something you can wear again," Lainey assures as she enters the conservatory where my mother, Meg, and I admire ourselves in a three-way mirror my mother hauled into the corner.

The three of us turn toward Lainey and gasp at the very same time.

"Lainey!" my mother cries out as she falls to her knees.

Okay, so that's a bit dramatic, but, my stars, somebody hold me because I swear on all that is holy I'm about to go down myself.

"Lainey!" My voice breaks as Meg and I stagger over. "You are so beautiful!"

Lainey beams like sunshine in a lightning white

dress, plunging neckline, cinched waist, belted with a blush pink ribbon, and a full skirt dripping with tulle.

The three of us scuttle over and wrap our arms around the gorgeous bride-to-be while losing ourselves in a vat of tears.

"Oh, Lainey"—my mother sobs—"you don't know how badly I wish your father were here to see this."

Lainey shrugs as she holds her hand out before us. "He sort of is."

A tiny blue heart sewn from the fabric of my father's dress shirt sits in her palm. It's the heart that my mother, Meg, and I gifted Lainey for her bridal shower last month.

"I'm going to tuck it into my bouquet like I said I would, but I wanted him here with me today, too."

We collapse over her once again with a firm embrace.

"Everything is about to change," Lainey mewls like a kitten.

Meg taps her on the shoulder. "For the better, Lainey. You and Forest are meant to be."

Lainey nods. "And so are you and Hook."

The three of them look my way.

"And...Mom and Mayor Nash are quite the swanky couple." Swanky? Is that somehow a derivative of the fact I think he's a wanker?

Mom waves it off. "Mayor Nash and I are currently

exploring other options." She looks as if she's about to be sick. "I'm sort of seeing Pastor Gaines."

"Mother!" Lainey smacks her on the arm three times fast, and Meg plucks poor Mom safely out of battering range. "How could you do this to me?"

I take a breath and close my eyes. "This might be a good time to mention that the wedding will no longer be held at its original venue." It's true. As soon as I recovered from the trauma of seeing Everett's back window beaten in, I found Naomi and asked her if she could do me a very big favor. Suffice it to say, I owe her one. Big time.

It takes everything I've got to pry a lid open as I force myself to look in my sister's direction.

Lainey's face bleaches as white as her dress. "Please tell me you're kidding." Her voice trembles with rage, and quite frankly it scares the daylights out of me.

"Actually"—I look to Meg for help, but she shakes her head as if she wants nothing to do with this bridal blunder—"I think the gazebo outside of the Evergreen Manor will be much more to your liking. And I have already procured Mom's new beau to officiate at the change of venue. Not to mention the fact I've put in an order with Felicity down at The Enchanted Flower Shop to have the gazebo covered in peonies."

Lainey sucks in a breath as if I just shot her.

"Should I have gone with roses?"

Lainey charges at me, and I brace for whatever she

might bring. But she doesn't deck me, or gouge my eyes out, or yank fistfuls of hair from my scalp. She hugs me as if I had just come back from the dead.

"You did it. You did the impossible."

"What?" I pull back, just to make sure she's still talking to me.

"Yes. It's what I really had my heart set on, but I vacillated, and as soon as the wheels got turning, I figured it was too late. But when I fantasize about saying my vows, I always envision Forest and me under a flower covered gazebo, and then I kick myself for being such a stickler on having it at the church."

I lift a shoulder her way. "Have pastor, will travel!"

The four of us break out into a warm laugh and then we break out into a dance as well. We sway to the rhythm of our love, of who we are, of who we're about to become. Best of all, we bathe in the depths of our love for one another.

Once the fitting ends, I hand my dress back to Scarlet Sage and head into the hall to say goodnight to my mother. But, instead of finding Miranda Lemon, I bump into another mother whom I did not expect to see.

"Carlotta. What are you doing here?"

Her hair is curled in soft waves, freshly dyed caramel brown, the exact shade of my own mane with nary a gray tendril in sight. Her face looks freshly scrubbed, and she's dressed to impress with a fitted black dress.

"Welcome to my new digs." She waves a hand through the air. "Becca got tired of me cramping her style, and Miranda was kind enough to offer me a room in exchange for light housekeeping duties."

A dull moan evicts from me. "You need to pay her something for rent."

She bats me away. "Oh hush, I will."

The roar of an all too familiar tiger growls from behind, and I turn to find little Lea in all her hairy glory holding Beasty by the tail. Before I can make my way over, a couple of disembodied spirits swoop in—Greer and Winslow—and they both look decidedly angry.

"What have you done to us?" Winslow cries out in what sounds like agony.

"Whatever do you mean?" I cringe as I glance back at Lea who seems to be barking out commands to Beasty, and the enormous creature seems more than happy to comply.

Greer grunts. "You know what we mean, Lottie. I told Winslow everything. Lea is running us ragged, bossing us around—shake this, howl at that. At the rate we're going, we'll extinguish ourselves just trying to keep pace."

"She's impossible," Winslow's voice echoes.

"She's far more than we can handle, Lottie. And now that you've put her in charge"—Greer looks to Winslow as if building up her nerve to say what comes next—"we're not sure if we can stay."

"What? No! You can't leave." I scurry forward as if hiding behind Greer in fear Lea will hear me. "Okay, listen. She helped me with—"

"With that boyfriend of yours," Lea finishes for me.

Here she is, front and center, a sour puss on her face so scary it could peel the paint off the wall, and if that curdling in the corner is any indication, it's already happening.

Winslow steps forward. "What exactly were the terms of your agreement?"

"I asked Lea to help bring Everett back safe and—"

Lea holds up a hand. "And if I did, she said she would put me in charge of haunting the B&B. I did and here we are. Now, why are the two of you slacking?" Her voice hikes to unnatural octaves.

Carlotta scoffs. "Wait a cotton pickin' bratty minute." Carlotta squints over at Lea. "Lottie and Noah figured out where the house was, they broke down the door, they hauled the man to safety. Exactly what role did you play in the matter?"

"Well, she…" I start in on her defense, then falter. "I mean, Beasty told us Everett was in the house."

"Beasty?" Carlotta cocks her head to the side. "It doesn't sound like little Lea was needed at all."

Lea's eyes widen with horror as she looks from me to Greer and Winslow.

"I won't have this," she shouts. "This is my house." Her voice breaks somewhere between a whimper and a whine. "This is my house, and I'll have it haunted *my* way." She stomps her foot and the floor rattles beneath me. "You just don't understand what it's like to be me!" She runs howling and screaming as every door in the B&B opens and slams shut at an alarming pace.

Greer scowls my way. "Now look what you've done to the poor girl."

Winslow cranes his neck in the direction she took off in. "I believe she needs a mother."

"And a father." Greer picks up his hand. "Come now. Let's find the little monster and hug it out. I think we're finally on our way to becoming a family." They float down the hall at record speed.

Beasty stretches out his front paws as if he just finished watching a movie, and I do believe everything he witnesses around here is highly entertaining.

"I'll be around when you need me, Lottie. But for now, I think it's best I go after my sweet little Lea." He trots off in their general direction, and I can't help but coo after him.

"That's adorable. Beasty is just as smitten by Lea as he was Jana."

"Yeah, so he's got a thing for dead girls," Carlotta smarts as she flattens the front of her dress. "How do I look?"

"Like the belle of the beastly ball. Where are you off to?"

"Harry is taking me to dinner tonight. He suggested I dress nice and I did."

"So the Jungle Room?" The Jungle Room is even seedier than the establishment it's buried in, and all sorts of kinky things go wrong in that place.

"I should be so lucky. He's taking us out for steaks by Honey Lake." Her phone bleats and she smirks at it. "Here goes nothing. Who knows, Lot? You might end up with a full-blooded baby brother or sister yet." A laugh rattles from her as she runs out the door.

So not funny.

And do you know what else isn't funny?

Lainey's wedding is in exactly three days.

Something tells me I'd better scour that wedding bible of Jana's before it's too late.

CHAPTER 19

*S*ince Lainey threatened us within an inch of our lives, neither Meg nor I was brave enough to steal her away to some dicey strip club that featured half-naked men. Instead, we took both her and Forest and everyone we know and booked the back room at Mangias and had an Italian feast fit for kings. Mom brought Pastor Gaines and Carlotta brought Mayor Nash, and, of course, I brought Noah and Everett.

Everett has taken to sleeping at his place again, and since I can't bear anything to happen to him, I packed up Pancake and Waffles and we've joined him. And since Noah is paranoid something will happen to *me*, he slept on Everett's couch last night. I, of course, opted for the sofa opposite him in an effort to keep things from getting any weirder among the three of us.

It's been exhausting trying to keep up with two different maniacs *and* stay one step ahead of Lainey's wedding.

Dinner was wonderful and everyone is mingling about the room as Sinatra booms from the speakers.

"Keelie"—I lean in toward my bestie—"what did Felicity say? Who else was in her apartment?"

She shakes her head. "No one."

"What? That doesn't make sense. Pages were ripped out of Jana's journal. We have proof. Someone must have broken in."

Bear comes over and steals Keelie away as they slowly rock together on the makeshift dance floor.

Figures. *Now* he's a hopeless romantic. But nonetheless, I'm thrilled for Keelie.

Meg bops up with Hook in tow as bodies move for the door.

"You ready, Lot?"

"I guess it's time. The wedding is in two days. It's going to be here in a blink of an eye. I still have to finish up the cake. I'm putting my all into it."

"I have no doubt. But I'm not talking about going home—consider yourself kidnapped."

"What?" I squawk just as Noah and Everett come up behind me.

Meg nods. "We're giving Lainey a ride home. Wink wink."

"Wink wink?"

"Yup. We'll be making a pit stop at the Ladies' Lounge. Don't worry, boys"—she grins over at Noah and Everett—"I'll have her home by three."

Noah and Everett exchange a glance.

The next thing I know, Lainey has a blindfold on, and Meg is speeding down the highway while Keelie and I sing a familiar song that happens to be playing on the radio at top volume.

"We can't seem to lose 'em, Lot!" Meg howls with a laugh as she looks to the car behind us.

"No, you won't. It's useless to even try," I say. Noah and Everett vowed to offer me a much-needed layer of protection tonight, and I wasn't about to turn them down. Heaven forbid Hailey show up and clobber me over the head, or worse yet, Lainey. Nope.

Noah and Everett have offered to make the supreme sacrifice—that of their male ego.

The Lady's Lounge is a hot pink mess that sits smack in the middle of the grimiest part of Leeds. Usually this is where I would let a wisecrack fly about how every part of Leeds is the grimiest part, but I would be oh so wrong.

"Oh my Lord," Lainey barks as soon as she takes off her blindfold. "Thank goodness Noah and Everett are with us. I can't believe Forest left me in your supervision. I'm seriously thinking of swapping out one of your boyfriends for the groom. And just to be clear, I'm talking to Lottie." She swats Meg with her purse as we're shuttled inside and greeted by the sound of twangy music that makes all sorts of pornographic promises.

The thick scent of cheap perfume engulfs us as throngs of women scream at the men swinging their stuff up on the long dark stage.

A barrage of neon lights rain down on a group of ten or twelve men, all gyrating their hips in time to one another. Much to my delight, they're all wearing jeans and a T-shirt—then in one well-choreographed move, their pants are torn away and they're currently working on getting rid of those T-shirts, too.

Meg scores a big round table down in front, and while she and Keelie lose their ever-loving minds screaming at the scantily clad men as if they were rock stars, Lainey and I sit back with Noah and Everett sipping on appletinis and noshing on French fries.

Noah leans in. "Don't ever say I never did anything for you, Lottie."

Everett shakes his head. "Cupcake, this is just a

preview before the main event. You and me, my bedroom. I've got a robe and a gavel."

Noah snorts. "I've got a badge and gun."

Lainey slumps my way. "Forest has a yellow trench coat and an axe. Can we leave now?"

Meg turns around. "Not on your life, Lainey Lemon. You do realize these are the last days of your life that anyone will ever call you that." She turns back around, hooting and hollering with the best of them while Lainey falls apart on my shoulder.

"Nothing will ever be the same again," Lainey laments as one set of naked men is traded for another.

"No, it won't. But that's the best part of all."

And the scariest, but I leave that little tidbit out.

THE DAY of Lainey's wedding, I get up at four in the morning—and for me, that's practically sleeping in. I pull my laptop forward in Everett's kitchen as I try not to wake anyone, but sweet Toby is front and center keeping me company like the loyal friend he is.

Hailey James.

I input her name into every search engine known to man and still come up empty.

Harlow James.

I try that one and the same sad stories bubble to the

top. I take my time and dig deeper and deeper and still nothing. I'm about to click out when I spot an errant article at the bottom of the page. *Dr. Isaac James donates one hundred thousand dollars to the Hampshire Psychiatric Hospital.*

I click over and hold my breath. *Dr. Isaac James donated to the facility for its exemplary care of his daughter who has been receiving long-term care within their department.*

His daughter? Could that be Hailey? It could have been Harlow for that matter. The article doesn't reference any names. I'm shocked they were allowed to print such sensitive information at all.

Footsteps liven behind me, and I close my laptop with a snap as I jump in my seat.

It's Everett. His hair is slightly mussed and he has that sexy glazed-over look in his eyes.

"I come in peace." He offers me a groggy half-smile and a kiss to the cheek. His breath is minty and I can't help but moan a little. "Are you ready for this day?"

"As ready as I'll ever be."

Everett takes up my hand and rubs that enormous rock over my ring finger.

"One day it will be your wedding, Lemon. You're going to make a beautiful bride."

"And you will make a lethally handsome groom. You don't suppose we'll be making that trek together, do you?"

His lips curl with a dangerous appeal. "Stranger things have happened." He takes me by the hand. Everett nods to the living room where Noah snores softly. "What's-his-face is still sleeping. And I'm in the mood to start the day with nice, long, hot shower."

"That sounds like heaven."

"It will be. Why don't we conserve a little water and hop in together?"

And we do.

WHEN MY SISTERS and I were little girls, we dressed up in my mother's wedding dress—a sin of the highest order that she must never know about—and pretended we were brides, taking turns marrying one another over and over again.

As we grew older, we longed for our happily ever afters even while kissing our fair share of horny toads.

When Lainey brought home Forest, everyone knew he was the one for her. And when they hit that unimaginable rough patch last summer, it was heart-wrenching to see them drift apart so violently. But then as fate, and Tanner Redwood's untimely death would have it, Forest and Lainey found their way back to one another. And here we are, all dressed and ready to go on the sprawling grounds of the Evergreen Manor.

Rows and rows of white ladder-back chairs have been set out, and a white aisle runner leads to the gazebo, which Felicity has turned into a magical lavender spectacle worthy of a million dollars—and that's pretty much what I paid for it, too. I wouldn't dare let Felicity give me that for free. She took it a step beyond the peonies and dusted it with baby's breath and purple wisteria as well. It gives the grounds a dreamy appeal, and I do my best to memorize how perfect everything is today.

This morning, as I got dressed, Noah presented me with a strange gift, a gun holster that wraps around my waist like a belt, only to link up to a smaller belt that circles my thigh. And yes, my gun sits nestled on the outer thigh of my right leg as if it's always belonged there. I suppose I could have protested the idea, but seeing that there will be a heck of a lot of people at this blessed event today, and that there is not one, but *two* deranged lunatics to keep an eye out for, I acquiesced without putting up a fight.

The sky is cobalt blue, the sun has yet to crest the woods, and the air holds the rich scent of heavenly flowers. The aisles, arches, and tabletops have all been ornately decorated with oodles and oodles of roses and peonies, lavender and pink just the way Lainey wanted.

The music starts up, and soon Meg and I are walked down the aisle with a couple of Forest's brothers.

I can't help but give a cheeky smile to both Noah and

Everett as I pass them. They both look so painfully dapper in their dark inky suits. Noah's tie is pale blue and Everett's is black as night.

Meg and I take our place up at the gazebo adorned with a waterfall of wisteria and baby's breath. It's a wonderland effect that gives this day a fairy-tale appeal.

Forest nods over to us, looking handsome as only a groom can be. He's wearing a gray suit, as are all of his groomsmen. One by one the rest of the wedding party makes its way over, and soon enough the tempo of the music changes and every last guest is on their feet facing the back. I even see Greer and Winslow and little Lea sitting on Beasty's shoulders. All of Honey Hollow—and even some from the other side have come out to see this love story hit its crescendo. But there is one person who couldn't be here today but very much should. And how I would move heaven and earth to make it so.

I close my eyes for a moment and envision my father, Joseph Lemon, in his prime. Tall, dark hair, eyes that say *I see you* and *you are special*, and an amazing smile to match. What a precious soul that man was. He only wanted to give the best to his girls, and my mother was always included in that equation. How I wish he could give us the best today—and that would be the honor of his presence.

The crowd gasps and I open my eyes to find my beautiful sister transformed into a glorious bride. Her hair is swept up, a simple strand of our grandmother's pearls grace her neck, her gown is immaculate, her bouquet so elegant, and it's even more special because it harbors that little piece of my father, the blue heart sewn together from his favorite dress shirt. My mother threads her arm through Lainey's, and a strange figure appears at Lainey's other side.

"What?" I whisper as I lean in and squint. "So help me if that's Mayor Nash," I mutter and Meg kicks me with her heel.

But it's not Mayor Nash. Slowly the form of a man appears, dressed in a tuxedo, his chin tucked in the air with pride, and my heart bottoms out as they step in closer.

The man is tall. He is both devastatingly handsome and familiar. A painful croak emits from my throat.

"Daddy?" It escapes from me faintly as tears stream down my face. Here he is, not alive, and certainly not in the flesh, but nonetheless he made it.

Joseph Lemon walks Lainey down the aisle and dots a gentle kiss to her cheek once he deposits her at Forest's feet. He steps over to my mother and pulls her in before landing a kiss to her lips, and, if I'm not mistaken, he's whispering something to her as well. He turns and walks my way. My legs turn to rubber, and it's all I can do to keep from leaping on him with a firm embrace.

He gifts Meg a kiss on the cheek before stepping in close to me.

"My little Lottie." He smiles that big familiar smile that always made me feel like the only girl in the world. "How I love you so." He lands a kiss to my cheek, and just like that, he evaporates to nothing.

Lainey and Forest exchange *I dos*, and before I know it, they're running down the aisle once again as the crowd breaks out into wild cheers. And it's done. Lainey and Forest have just crossed over into their happily ever after.

Noah and Everett come my way.

"You did great, Lottie." Noah takes my hand and lands a kiss to the back.

Everett nods. "Lemon, you look dangerously gorgeous in that dress. I get the first dance."

"Done." I spot Jackie stepping into the back of the Evergreen ballroom. "Would you two excuse me? There's one more thing I need to supervise, and Lord knows nothing can go wrong today."

"Sure thing." Noah points toward the woods. "Ivy's here. I thought we might need extra eyes on the grounds."

"Good thinking. And she's more than welcome at the reception."

I take off and bump into a body as soon as I get through the door.

"Lottie"—Hook catches me before I sail into a wall— "whoa. Careful there." He lets go and backtracks before I can head into the next room. "Hey, I did a little research, and Underwood Investments is indeed a huge enterprise. The strange thing is, I couldn't find any satellites. Do me a favor, and keep your money far away from that outfit. I'm going to investigate further sometime next week."

"Yeah, sure. No worries. My money isn't going anywhere." I stride into the ballroom and the sight of all the beautiful tables takes my breath away. I've been in here all afternoon, but it's not until now that the lights have been dimmed and the magic of the twinkle lights has taken over. It's beyond beautiful and tears come to my eyes once again. In the corner, the cake I worked on gleams under the duress of this low lighting—three lavender tiers, each tinged with thick gold icing dripping down the sides, exactly the way Lainey wanted. It looks amazing if I do say so myself.

"Hey, Lottie!" Jackie waves from the front near the head table with a luxurious spread of flowers cascading over it. "What do you think?" She thumps her hand over one of the Grecian columns set to either side of the table.

"I think it's sheer perfection. I know Jana would be proud of it. Lainey will love it, too."

Pierce comes up beaming with a smile. "It took a little grunt work, but we got it done." He slips his arm around Jackie's waist, and I can't help but think it looks a touch invasive, intimate.

"Yes, you did. Thank you so much. Hey, I was talking

to Steven a bit ago, and I've thought about what he said. I'm ready to invest my money." My heart thumps wildly. This is hardly the venue to keep pecking away at suspects, but I can't help it. It's what I was born to do.

His brows arch. "That's fantastic. Swing by the office anytime, and Steven will set you right up. Don't worry, Lottie. Your money will be in safe hands. You're making the right decision." He pats Jackie on the bottom. "I left some tools out by the kitchen. I'll be right back." He takes off, and I watch as she blows him a kiss.

My word, they're not even hiding it anymore.

My heart sinks as the DJ starts playing a little mood music.

"Lainey and Forest have gone to the falls with the photographer," I say. "It's only five minutes away, and they're going to take a few couple's shots and come right back. I don't have my purse with me, but I'd love to pay you for your time." My throat grows scratchy from the lie.

"*Please*—just bring another box of those delicious donuts to the office the next time you swing by, and we'll call it even."

"Consider it done. I guess, in the meantime, I'll go online and check out your website."

She averts her eyes as she leans in. "We don't have a website per se. That's actually another Underwood Investments. We get mistaken for them all the time. Truthfully, I think that's why our clients are so quick to use us. But Pierce knows what he's doing. I have all my spare change locked up with them. It's a good place. Welcome to the family, Lottie."

"Thank you," I say stiffly as I watch her finish polishing the columns.

I head out and spot Hook once again. "Hook!" I prance my way over as fast as my kitten heels will allow. "Jackie just fessed up." I spill quickly what she mentioned about the website.

"I knew it." He slaps his thigh. "That's called a cheater brand. Pierce is riding on the coattails of someone else's hard work. I knew as soon as you said binary investments this was a crooked setup. Stay the heck away. You hear me? I'm going to talk to Noah about investigating them for fraud. If I'm right, they're not investing much into commodities as they are into their own bank accounts. No wonder the guy is rolling around town in every luxury car known to man. He's nothing but a swindler."

I take off for the back, determined to find Noah or Everett to share the news.

"Lottie!" Meg comes crashing my way. "Lainey just texted and said to make sure line item fifty-seven is taken care of by the time they get back. What was line item fifty-seven?"

"Line item fifty-seven? Crap." I pick up the skirt of my dress. "I've got the wedding bible in my car. I'll be right back." I make a beeline for my beat-up hatchback and get all the way there when I realize my purse is somewhere in the changing room upstairs. Oh heck, it's a good thing my mother slapped a hide-a-key on this jalopy many Christmases ago, as she did for my sisters as well. Once my dad passed away, my mother became both mother and father to us, and this is just another example of her taking care of us.

I pause a moment to soak in the fact my dear sweet father was indeed here to walk Lainey down the aisle. It was heartbreakingly amazing, and equally agonizing because I was the only person on this side of the great divide who was able to witness the event—well, outside of Carlotta, if she noticed at all.

I pluck the key out from the wheel well and have that wedding bible in my hands in no time. I crack it right open to the center and trace my finger down the list, but it ends at fifty-six.

What?

Wait a minute. I tip my head back.

I think this just might be Lainey's way of getting back at us for the naughty nightie party—which Forest should be penning me a thank you for—or for that raucous night out at the Lady's Lounge, or perhaps even for a change of venue.

"Well played, Lainey Donovan. Well played."

A few pages slip out the side of the enormous tomb. I catch them in the air and gasp at the sight.

In my hands I hold the missing pages to Jana's journal. Every last one of them.

My heart thumps like a jackrabbit as I plop the wedding bible back onto the driver's seat and I read as fast as my eyes will allow.

Oh my stars.

Nobody broke in and ripped these pages out of her diary. Jana tore them out herself—in the event something horrible was about to happen to her. And she put them in the very place she knew someone would look.

And now I know her secret.

I know exactly why Jana March was killed.

CHAPTER 20

*I*t was right there under my nose, literally—
the answer I was so desperately seeking. I
suppose it's that way with many things, all of those
aches that clutter my heart. But when you don't know
where to look or that the answer lies less than an arm's
length away, you struggle for a solution—and sometimes, in the end, that helps paint a clearer picture.

A quick visual scan of the parking lot doesn't avail a single soul I'm looking for.

I send a quick group text to Noah and Everett and ask them to meet me at the gazebo.

There are still so many questions, so many unanswered reasons why Jana had to die. Was what I read reason enough? If the answer is self-preservation of the killer, then yes, it was more than reason enough.

I'm about to lock up my car when I spot Jackie and Pierce closing up the trunk of a cargo van. I jog over in hopes to clarify a few things before they leave.

"Hey!" Jackie waves. "We're taking off. And I meant what I said. Bring those donuts and we'll take care of everything else. In fact, I'll knock fifty percent off Steven's fee. Don't tell him I said so." She winks at Pierce before patting her hips down. "Shoot. I left my keys in the ballroom. I'll be right back."

She bolts off and I take a few careful steps in close to him. My heart thumps wildly and my adrenaline picks up.

He tips his head to the side as our eyes lock. Yes, Pierce is a very handsome man, muscular, exorbitantly wealthy. I can see why women would give him whatever he wanted, why some would give him their dignity.

"What's going on, Lottie?" His expression deadens as if he knew what I had found, what I know.

"Noah and Everett are on their way over," I say for

no reason other than the fact I felt I needed to. I pull out my phone and click over to the group chat.

"What are you looking at?" He comes over close, his arms menacingly crossed, and I quickly clutch the phone to my chest.

"Nothing. I was just checking my messages." I start to walk backward. "So, will I see you at the office next week? Jackie is right. I'm bringing donuts." A weak laugh emits from me.

His eyes remain trained on mine as he continues to walk my way, my feet never slowing as I try to slowly head back to the manor.

"I'd better go. They're going to come looking for me," I say.

"I'm sure they will." His brows pull into a line, and it looks intimidating. I'm sure it's meant to be. "So it's true? You're the best?"

"The best what?" I shake my head as my dress catches my eye. "Maid of honor! You're right. I'd better get back." I try to circle around him, but he blocks my path.

"Best at hunting down a killer." A laugh rattles in his chest, low and threatening like a thunderstorm looming on the horizon.

"You killed her? You killed Jana?" I shake my head as I continue to make my way backward. "Because of what? The fact she overheard a conversation?"

He closes his eyes for a brief moment. "So you do know."

I suck in a quick breath. "It's true. You're running some silly scam and Jana found out about it. She heard you and Steven having an argument about sales. And for that you killed her?" She also said she was through with him, and that as soon as my sister's wedding was over she would dump him—but not before she went to the police. Sweet Jana didn't want anything making waves for Lainey's wedding—not even her own broken heart.

"Silly scam?" He barks out a laugh. "That silly scam is a felony offense. If anyone had gotten wind of it, I'd be sitting in a penitentiary instead of on a yacht come next week."

We hit the edge of the woods, and I glance back to the Evergreen Manor, a speck compared to what it was.

I'm not going into the woods. I've played this game one too many times before. My body instantly drenches in sweat. I can feel the gun hot against my thigh, begging me to pick it up. But Pierce is strong. He can overpower me in the same way I've been overpowered in the past. That gun was used against me once before and I was lucky that it didn't kill me, but I'm not feeling so lucky anymore.

A spear of light blinds me from the west, and I spot Beasty bounding over, Lea on his back spurring him on by kicking her heels into his sides. It's always nice to see the supernatural cavalry arrive, even if it signals the end of their stay—Beasty's at least. I have no idea how to keep my promise to him.

"So you're leaving the country?" A laugh gets buried in my throat. "That should have been my tip-off. The killer always leaves the country." In the movies at least.

"And you would have been wrong," a female voice projects from my right, and I find Jackie strutting over with an enormous tote bag slung over her shoulder. "I lured Jana to the back of the convention center." She shrugs. "What can I say? He's my boss. He tells me what to do and I do it."

I can't help but scoff. "Some best friend."

"I *was* her best friend," she grits it through her teeth. "I stopped Pierce from putting a hit on her. And, believe me, they weren't going to be as humane as I was able to be."

"You could have gone to the sheriff's department." I shake my head in disbelief.

"And what? Had a hit out on me, too? No thanks. I lured Jana to the back, yes, but when push came to shove, I didn't think I could pull the trigger." She looks to Pierce. "That's why he had Steven meet up with us just as we left the building. I guess you could say I needed a cheerleader. I pulled the gun out. I had only used it once before. I didn't think I could do it. But I had to. Jana wasn't safe. She wanted to go to the police. She couldn't keep us safe." She shudders as she slides the tote bag off her shoulder. "Anyway, things are starting to look up for me. I've got a new best friend." She looks to Pierce. "And he's pretty good in bed, too."

So that's the benefit she got for killing Jana—Pierce. Something tells me Jackie was just looking for an excuse, and Pierce presented the perfect setup. Jackie believed she had to do it to save her own life. I'm sure she further justified it by thinking Jana would have done the same. But Jana wouldn't have. Not in a million years.

"Knew it." A choking sound emits from me. "I hope you know you're still sharing him. Monica Peeler," I say, looking at Pierce. "She's your side girl, right? That's what your sister told me."

His eyes harden dark as stones. "I knew you were snooping around. You stupid little—"

Something solid and hard whacks me on the side of the head, and I land face-first in a bed of pine needles.

I look up groggily to find Jackie hoisting that tote bag back over her shoulder.

"Let's get out of here." She tugs at his hand, but Pierce is immovable.

"We're not leaving her here to snitch."

"So what?" Jackie's voice rides high in a panic. "We can have the plane ready in ten minutes. We were leaving anyway."

They were leaving? Together? I bet they were about to stiff Steven with the felonious bag.

I go to move and my head feels like a bowling ball. The gun grazes against my thigh and I carefully reach down and slide it out of its holster. The memory of the blowback comes to mind, and I gird myself even though I'm nowhere near firing it.

"We're not killing her." Jackie yanks at his arm.

"We're sure as hell not leaving her. I can't risk it."

"Exactly!" she roars in his face.

Beasty slinks up. "Avenge my sweet Jana now or so help me heaven, I will do it myself." He belts out a ferocious roar, and it spurs me to jump to my feet.

"Lottie"—Lea calls out—"aim low for the man. He deserves a solid hit." Her eyes burn like fire, and it adds a frightening appeal to her already, well, frightening appeal.

I lift the gun toward Pierce, and my hands shake hard.

Jackie turns my way, and her mouth opens—to warn Pierce—to scream—I don't know which because I fire.

Pierce bucks and staggers backward, holding his stomach as Lea shouts out a wild cheer.

Beasty roars as he races his way and stomps over Pierce's chest. "Wasn't fatal. Try again."

"What?" I look to Jackie as she places her hands in the air. She's walking backward, and I can see the need to run in her eyes.

"Lottie!" Noah shouts and I hear what sounds like the stampeding of wild horses headed in this direction.

Noah and Everett and Ivy, too. I can see them in my peripheral vision.

"Let me go," Jackie pleads. "Lottie, let's turn Pierce

and Steven in together. Nobody has to know our secret. I was trapped. I had no choice. You have no proof I killed Jana. I'll say it's their word against mine. Please, forget everything you heard. Do it for Jana. I'm begging you."

"I will. I will do it for Jana," I say just as Ivy barks at Jackie to put her hands up and fall to her knees. "She killed her." I nod to Jackie. "And trust me, I did that for Jana because I was a real friend to her."

Noah lands hard over Pierce and cuffs him, ignoring the fact he's already moaning on the ground.

"Jackie killed Jana. Steven and Pierce were in on it," I pant as Everett collapses his arms around me. He takes the gun from my shaky hands and lands a kiss on the top of my head.

"It's over." Everett warms me with his body as Beasty makes his way toward us.

"Good work," he thunders it out like a threat. It's clear he's still as worked up as I am.

Lea's eyes sparkle a strange shade of crimson, and it's unnerving. "I want another murder in Honey Hollow. I want another killer to catch, and I want it now!"

Greer and Winslow appear from nowhere, and Greer takes up the little girl's hand.

"Is that any way to talk, young lady?" Greer is quick to scold her. "We do not wish homicides on the good people of Honey Hollow. I'm afraid you'll have to go to your room and think about that for a while."

"Do I have to?" Lea whines to Winslow.

"I think it's best," he says with a wink. "I'll join you and we'll play knock the books off the shelf."

"That is my very favorite game."

They wave my way as the three of them dissipate to nothing.

I meet up with Everett's sky-blue eyes. "And now that's what you call a family."

Beasty roars as he begins to dissipate as well.

"No, no." I traipse over, my hand still holding tight to Everett. "I'm not ready for you to go, Beasty." I run my hand over his fur, and it feels like a fine silk rug from the Orient. "I'm so sorry I couldn't keep my promise to you."

"I've changed my mind. I'm going willingly. I need to comfort my sweet Jana. I'll be back someday. Perhaps sooner than later." His head rolls in a soft circle. "Your powers are growing. I'm thankful for all you've allowed. Be well." A magnificent spray of light infiltrates the very spot he was standing in, and everyone in the vicinity winces.

Ivy blinks back. "That's quite a sunset."

"Yes," I whisper with a touch of grief. "I suppose we should get back to the wedding."

Ivy chuckles. "We'll need you downtown for questioning, Lemon. Sorry, but that's procedure."

"Procedure can wait," Noah says, lifting Pierce to his feet. "Enjoy your family, Lottie. You deserve it."

Everett and I head back toward the Evergreen Manor, and I intend to enjoy every blissful moment.

I wrap my arms around him as we make the lazy trek back.

"I love you so much, Lemon." He drops a kiss to my cheek. "I need you to know that."

It sounds far darker than it ever does romantic, and just as I'm about to look into his gorgeous eyes and question him, a heavy thud emits to our left.

"Did you hear that?" I tip my head toward the sea of cars. The sun has set, the light is murky, but I spot a figure crouched next to an all too familiar sedan as a baseball bat rises into the air. "Oh my goodness, it's her. That's your car." I snatch the gun from his hands and bolt without putting in a second thought.

Everett is willing to do just about anything to a woman—with her consent, of course—but shooting them isn't one of those things. But I'm not above putting a bullet in this maniac's body. I'll do whatever it takes to stop her. I haven't killed a person yet, but I'm not taking it off the table either.

Everett's forceful footfalls line up with mine. "Stop," he hisses, his phone already in his right hand as he does his best to alert Noah I'm presuming.

But I'm not listening to Everett. In fact, the only thing I hear is the sound of my heartbeat detonating in my ears, one bionic boom at a time.

"Freeze!" I roar as I come up within thirty feet of her.

The woman turns around, the look of surprise rife on her face. It's the brunette I saw last month, the one with the gorgeous bone structure and the breathtaking good looks that could stun a stranger into submission.

"It's you," I pant. "Hailey James."

A pained smile spreads over her face. "This is how you repay me, Essex? With *her*? What do you see in this simple girl?" She shakes her head with disgust written over her face. "She's plain, dull, there isn't a spark of life in her. I have everything you could ever want. Just come with me." She holds out her left hand, the bat still firmly secured in her right. "We could have our baby back. We could have everything. Let's leave this world behind and make our own. We have the funding. We can have everything we've ever wanted. The baby. She waits for us. She needs us to make her happen."

"Put down your weapon and I won't shoot," I shout as Everett walks around me. "Everett, don't move. She'll use you to her advantage. She's not going anywhere on my watch."

"Hailey, put the bat down," he coaxes. "We'll get some pizza and talk it over like old times, right? I miss our talks. Do you miss them, too?"

My stomach sinks as if there was a thread of truth in that, but I know there isn't. Everett is just that believable right now, and I'm thankful for it.

"Yes," she hisses as tears come to her eyes. "I miss

everything about us. Come to me, please," she beckons as she extends her hand farther his way.

Everett eyes it, and I can tell he's determined to take a chance in hopes to disarm her himself. He goes for her hand and she swings the bat—and I don't hesitate to shoot. Her body falls backward as the bat flies wildly through the air. She's clutching her shoulder as Noah runs over and the two of them help get her hands behind her back. Noah pulls a zip tie out of his pocket.

"I'm all out of cuffs." He looks my way. "With you around, I might need to carry extra."

Everett comes my way, and this time it's me wrapping my arms tightly around him.

"And now it's really over," I whisper.

Noah gets her to her feet as she grunts out in pain. The sound of patrol cars wailing their way over lights up the air.

I take a bold step forward, toward this lunatic who's been making our lives a living hell. "You're not really Hailey, are you?"

Her eyes widen as she looks from Everett to me. "How do you know?"

"Your father donated a large sum of money to the hospital that was looking after you for the last six years. You never had Everett's baby inside your body. You just wanted him then, like you do now. You lied about everything."

"I didn't lie." A husky laugh emits from her as blood

pools over her tan blouse. "My car fell off an icy embankment. They accused me of trying to take my own life! It wasn't true! We could still have that baby. I wasn't done with Essex." She looks his way. "I'll never be through with you." Her voice grows small as she collapses in Noah's arms.

Everett and I watch as the sheriff's department loads Pierce and Jackie away. An ambulance picks up Hailey —*Harlow* as it were, and Noah promises she's not getting away. He'll be watching her himself. We watch as the barrage of patrol cars and the siren of the ambulance disappear back out of sight as if none of it had happened. And just like that, it all feels like a faraway dream.

Everett presses a tired kiss over my lips. "Do they still do the YMCA at weddings?"

"I don't know, but I think we should go find out."

"If they do, I'm sitting that one out."

"How about a slow dance?"

"How about a slow dance in a dark office with just you and me?"

I bite down on a smile. "Things have been known to get pretty heated when the two of us are left to our own devices in just about any office space."

"That's what I'm wishing for, Lemon."

"Brace yourself, Judge Baxter. I'm about to make all of your wishes come true."

We head back, and I clean myself up for pictures. We

enjoy an elegant dinner catered by the Honey Pot Diner and watch as Lainey and Forest feed one another pink champagne cake in an indelicate manner. It's all in fun—all in love.

Everett and I enjoy the first dance with the lucky couple, and as soon as the Village People belt out their famous anthem, Everett whisks me away down a dark hall, into a small cubicle that has nothing more than a flimsy curtain dividing us from the roaming public. I get the feeling Everett likes a hint of danger with his desire.

And I give him all of the desire I have for him. We burn up that tiny glorified closet. We burn up the Evergreen Manor with our greedy need to fulfill our darkest desires.

And just like that, it's a wedding to remember.

CHAPTER 21

he Honey Pot Diner is filled to the brim with just about everyone we know. That's the beauty of Honey Hollow. It's nearly impossible to go somewhere and not run into someone you grew up with, a family member, a friend. I wouldn't want it any other way.

It's several days after the wedding, and Lainey and

Forest are up north, enjoying their special time as newlyweds at the gorgeous resort my new half-brother, Finn, runs.

Harlow was arraigned today. She pleaded not guilty by reason of insanity—and her father popped back into the picture, wagging documentation to prove it. Everett assured me she isn't going anywhere—and I'm resting assured in his words.

Jackie, Pierce, and Steven will be arraigned tomorrow. Everett gave us the heads-up that they're pleading guilty. Pierce agreed to tell them everything he knows about the crooked dealings of his company in hopes to get a lesser charge in the arena. Nevertheless, they should probably get comfortable behind bars. They're going to be there a good long while.

It was my idea to take both Noah and Everett to dinner. Now that we're all settled in our respective homes once again, it feels as if we hardly see each other. Lord knows I miss Toby, and so do Pancake and Waffles.

Keelie is the first to greet us as we walk through the door.

"Everyone is here!" She gifts me one of her gigantic hugs. "I'll set a table up for the three of you. Just give me a second." She steps away before bouncing back. "Oh, and Lottie? No stumbling upon any dead bodies tonight, okay? Bear is taking me to the overlook later, and we're going to watch for shooting stars."

"That's so romantic! But don't tell him I said so. I'd hate to ruin his mojo in that department."

"Believe me, Lottie, nothing is going to ruin what we have." She takes off, and a cold chill runs through me as I turn to Noah and Everett.

"I believed that once, too." I shrug up at Noah, and he pulls me in for a partial hug.

"I'm betting everything works out in the end."

"It will," Everett assures as he takes up my hand. "I spoke to my mother today. She says she insists on giving both you and Noah the reward money. One hundred thousand dollars, split down the middle for ensuring my safe return. She wants to make the deposit into your bank accounts as soon as possible."

My mouth falls open at the thought.

Noah shakes his head. "No way. Lottie can have it all."

"No." I'm quick to forfeit the funds. "I don't want it. Please tell your mother that it was a very nice gesture, but I'm happy just having you here safe."

"I'm afraid she won't take no for an answer."

"It's true." Noah chuckles. "Once she gets her mind set to something, there's no stopping her. Come to think of it, she reminds me a lot of you."

"Well, then, why don't we have her donate the money?" My heart thumps hard just thinking of how much money that is. "To the hospital?"

"The children's ward?" Noah suggests.

"Yes!" I turn to Everett. "The children's ward would be perfect. If that's all right with you, that would be my request."

"That's more than all right with me." Everett lands a kiss to my forehead. "I'll tell her first thing."

The door chimes behind us and in stumble two bumbling blondes. Okay, so just one bumbling blonde. The other one is just maniacal.

"Cormack, Britney." I nod their way.

Britney looks stunning tonight, and I hate to admit it, but perhaps the best I've ever seen her.

"I'm meeting with a friend." She looks to Noah. "May I speak with you for a minute?"

"Sure." Noah doesn't hesitate to give his wife the attention she craves—as he should.

"Finally." Everett watches as they head back out into the Honey Hollow night before turning my way. "Noah's younger brother contacted me this morning."

"Alex!" Cormack hops up and down, her head bouncing as if it's on springs. "Oh, I just love that boy to death!"

Everett lifts his chin, amused. "Yes, well, that boy is an ex-Marine turned investment banker, and he's coming out here in a couple of weeks. He wants to throw his brother a surprise birthday party."

Cormack hops up and down again as she slowly

makes the transformation from human to pogo stick. "A birthday party! A birthday party!"

"It's a *surprise* party," I say with my voice as low as a whisper, hoping she'll follow suit. "Which usually means you don't chant about it when you're less than six feet from the guest of honor." It's true. Noah might have his back to us, but we can still see him. I turn to Everett. "That's fantastic! When and where? Of course, I'll bake the cake."

"That's just it. He left it up to me, and I was hoping you'd help out in that department. His only request was that it take place the first Saturday of August."

"His birthday isn't until almost the end of the month, but I can understand that. And this way it will be a total surprise. We can have it at my place," I'm quick to volunteer my adorable rental.

"Your place?" Cormack shoves her tiny fists to her hips. "We're not having some house party for my fiancé. Oh no, no, no. This shall be a grand soiree. I'm thinking the ballroom at the Evergreen Manor."

I'm quick to frown at the idea. Noah is far more laid-back.

"How about Honey Lake?" I offer. "The Honey Festival lasts all next month. And every weekend there's a band and lots of food. It's practically begging for a birthday party."

Cormack lifts her hands to her mouth as if she were praying.

"They have fireworks every Saturday night," I add, trying to get her on board, and I'm not exactly sure why. "I'll reserve an area for us with picnic tables." I blink up at Everett. "What kind of cake do you think Noah would like?"

"He's an officer of the law. I suspect donuts are in order."

"A cake made entirely out of donuts! Perfect. Consider it done."

The door chimes and in walks my mother, Mayor Nash, and Kelleth.

"Lottie!" Mom pulls me into a quick embrace. "Every time I think of you, I'm fearing for the worst. You really know how to give your poor mother a scare."

"And your father." Mayor Nash flashes his politician smile, but I'm not smiling along with him. He sobers up rather quickly. "If you don't mind, Lottie, I would still love for us to get together sometime to chat. Sort of catch up on things, if you will."

"I'd like that." I glance to my mother, silently questioning what she's still doing with him.

Mom leans in and whispers, "Carlotta and Pastor Gaines are on their way. It's our first double date." She squeezes her eyes shut with excitement, and I don't bother asking who is dating who—or bother defining double date since we've got an extra body on hand. "Oh, and before I forget, Lainey just told me their offer was accepted. They move in as soon as escrow closes in a couple of weeks!"

"That's so great!" I say as she hugs Mayor Nash and they conduct their own private celebration. Awkward. It's nice to see she's fully over him.

Kelleth tosses her blonde mane back. "Steven was arrested. Are you satisfied?"

"I'm sorry." I blink her way. "But I guess the sheriff's department deemed that he was involved in something illegal." And, seeing that he was an accessory to murder, I'd say he certainly was.

"Yes, well, I'm being investigated, too. Not only that, but I'm out of a job. I'll have to resort to that treachery my sister subjects herself to."

My lids flash wide open. I happen to remember that Aspen works for the Elite Entourage, which is essentially a high-class call girl service. Note to self: Have a little chat with your sisters regarding poor career choices and the consequences that can haunt them for a lifetime.

The three of them are quickly seated as Everett, Cormack, and I wait patiently for Noah.

Everett leans in and brushes a kiss over my ear. "Did you know we can see all the shooting stars we want off the widow's walk on my rooftop?"

A dark laugh brews in my chest. "Oh honey, we don't need to go that far. I can see all the stars I want, right there in your bedroom. In fact, I do believe you've shown me a few new constellations or two."

The tips of his lips curl with devilish intent. "What do you say we wrap this up early and shoot for the stars?"

"I think this night is bound to end in an out-of-this-world experience."

Noah opens the door and lets Britney step inside first. He walks over and takes a deep breath, his ever-green eyes never leaving mine.

"Lottie, Everett." Noah is charged. There's a spark in his eyes that I haven't seen in a very long time. "I've asked Britney to relay something to you."

Britney tips her head, and a long silky wave of creamy blonde hair covers one eye as if it held a secret.

Britney's pouty lips pump a short-lived smile. "I've made the decision to proceed with the divorce. If all goes well, the papers should be final sometime next month. Now, if you'll excuse me, I've got a table reserved for two. I'm expecting your brother, Finn, at any moment." She takes off deeper into the restaurant and leaves my jaw on the floor.

For a while now, having Noah tangled up in a marital nightmare has been my saving grace in a way. But now it feels as if the floodgates have opened, and all hell is about to break loose inside of me. I'm more confused than ever. Yes, I'm dating Everett, but Noah and I have a history—and despite Britney, it's one I look upon fondly.

Noah looks to Everett with an ice-cold stare. "You heard her. My divorce will be final in weeks. Should we tell her?"

I inch back, glancing briefly at Cormack who's staring vacantly at her phone a few feet away. "Tell *me*? Tell me what?"

Noah nods. "Everett and I had a nice long talk this morning—before I knew anything about Britney's surprise. He agreed it's only fair that you explore your feelings for me."

My heart gives a violent wallop as Everett indulges in a long blink.

"It's true, Lemon. I don't want to hold you back if you have very real feelings for him. It's time to shut that door forever before we can move on to the next phase." He picks up my hand and touches that rock on my finger. "I want you to be certain. No regrets."

No regrets.

I take a deep breath as Keelie bounces over and seats us for dinner—a dinner I'm already regretting.

Everett is loosening his grip over my heart to see if I'll fly away to someone else.

Noah is hoping I'll return to him.

Both Noah and Everett have my love and both would like to have it fully.

And once the ink is dry on Noah's divorce, it's open season on my heart.

I can't see a single thing that can go wrong with this. Mostly.

*Pick up Donut Disaster (Murder in the Mix 12) TODAY!**

RECIPE

Champagne Wedding Cake
From the Cutie Pie Bakery and Cakery

*H*ello! Lottie here! Well guess who got a new brother-in-law? This girl! I can't believe my sister, Lainey, and Forest finally tied the knot. I can't tell you how happy I am for them both. And it was one of the biggest honors of my life to bake the wedding cake for them. The minute Lainey and I put our heads together we came up with this ultra-lux, ultra-delicious confection. We hope you'll love it as much as we do. There wasn't a single bite left at the end of the reception. This cake is a hit for just about any occasion.

Have fun with it!

Ingredients Pink Champagne Cake

3 cups flour

1 cup butter (2 sticks, unsalted, softened)

1 ¾ cups sugar

6 egg whites

1 cup pink champagne (any brand will do)

1 tablespoon baking powder

2 tablespoons vegetable oil

2 teaspoons vanilla

½ teaspoon salt

7-9 drops red food coloring to create a pink hue

Ingredients Pink Champagne Buttercream

1 cup unsalted butter (room temperature)

4-5 cups powdered sugar

¼ cup pink champagne

2 teaspoons vanilla extract

A pinch of salt

¼ teaspoon pink gel color or 3-5 drop red food coloring

Directions Pink Champagne Cake

Bake at 350° F

Prepare two 9 inch round baking pans by spraying them with cooking oil or rubbing them down with butter.

In a stand mixer with a paddle attachment (or a large

bowl with a hand mixer) add butter and sugar, creaming them together (3 -5 minutes).

In a medium bowl combine flour, baking powder, and salt. Whisk and set aside.

In another medium bowl combine egg whites, champagne, oil, food coloring, and vanilla.

Alternate adding the dry flour mixture and the wet champagne mixture into the mixing bowl with the creamed butter and sugar. Work slowly until ingredients are combined then increase speed to medium to blend well (about two minutes).

Pour batter into the cake pans and bake for 25-30 minutes until a toothpick comes out clean from the center. Let cool for 15 minutes before ready to frost.

Directions Pink Champagne Buttercream

*The paddle attachment on the stand mixer works for this, but a handheld mixer works well, too.

Beat butter until smooth and creamy for about two minutes. Add four cups of powdered sugar, champagne, vanilla extract, and a pinch of salt. Beat on high for about two minutes. If the consistency is too thin, add more powdered sugar until desired consistency is achieved.

BOOKS BY ADDISON MOORE

Murder in the Mix Mysteries
Cutie Pies and Deadly Lies
Bobbing for Bodies
Pumpkin Spice Sacrifice
Gingerbread & Deadly Dread
Seven-Layer Slayer
Red Velvet Vengeance
Bloodbaths and Banana Cake
New York Cheesecake Chaos
Lethal Lemon Bars
Macaron Massacre
Wedding Cake Carnage
Donut Disaster
Toxic Apple Turnovers
Killer Cupcakes
Pumpkin Pie Parting
Yule Log Eulogy
Pancake Panic
Sugar Cookie Slaughter
Devil's Food Cake Doom

Snickerdoodle Secrets

Strawberry Shortcake Sins

Cake Pop Casualties

Flag Cake Felonies

Peach Cobbler Confessions

Poison Apple Crisp

Spooky Spice Cake Curse

Pecan Pie Predicament

Eggnog Trifle Trouble

Waffles at the Wake

Raspberry Tart Terror

Baby Bundt Cake Confusion

Chocolate Chip Cookie Conundrum

Wicked Whoopie Pies

Key Lime Pie Perjury

Red, White, and Blueberry Muffin Murder

Honey Buns Homicide

Apple Fritter Fright

Vampire Brownie Bite Bereavement

Pumpkin Roll Reckoning

Cookie Exchange Execution

Heart-Shaped Confection Deception

Birthday Cake Bloodshed

Cream Puff Punishment

Last Rites Beignet Bites

For a full list please visit Addisonmoore.com

ACKNOWLEDGMENTS

Thank YOU so much for spending time in Honey Hollow! I hope you enjoyed the adventure with Lottie and all of her Honey Hollow peeps as much as I did. The MURDER IN THE MIX mysteries are so very special to me, and I hope they are to you as well. If you'd like to be in the know on upcoming releases, please be sure to follow me at Bookbub and Amazon. Simply click the links on the next page. I am SUPER excited to share the next book with you! So much happens and so much changes. Thank you from the bottom of my heart for taking this wild roller coaster ride with me. I really do love you!

A big thank you to Kaila Eileen Turingan-Ramos and Jodie Tarleton. You ladies rock my world.

A very special shout-out to my fabulous betas, Shay Rivera, Lisa Markson, Anastasia Lantilou Steele and Ashley Marie Daniels. Thank you so much for your valuable time!

A special thanks to Lou Harper of Cover Affairs! You are the best of the best, and I am forever grateful that you are sharing your talent with the world.

And thank you to the amazing, supercalifragilisticexpialidocious Paige Maroney Smith for spanking this novel into submission. You are the best of the best. There are none like you!

And last, but never least, thank you to Him who sits on the throne. Worthy is the Lamb! Glory and honor and power are yours. I owe you everything, Jesus.

ABOUT THE AUTHOR

Addison Moore is a *New York Times, USA TODAY,* and *Wall Street Journal* bestselling author. Her work has been featured in *Cosmopolitan* Magazine. Previously she worked as a therapist on a locked psychiatric unit for nearly a decade. She resides on the West Coast with her husband, four wonderful children, and two dogs where she eats too much chocolate and stays up way too late. When she's not writing, she's reading. Addison's Celestra Series has been optioned for film by **20th Century Fox.**

Made in the USA
Columbia, SC
03 September 2024

41399750R00159